I0661894

Frederic Beecher Perkins

The Picture and the Men

Frederic Beecher Perkins

The Picture and the Men

ISBN/EAN: 9783337375959

Printed in Europe, USA, Canada, Australia, Japan

Cover: Foto ©Andreas Hilbeck / pixelio.de

More available books at **www.hansebooks.com**

THE PICTURE

AND

THE MEN:

BEING —

BIOGRAPHICAL SKETCHES OF PRESIDENT LINCOLN AND HIS
CABINET; TOGETHER WITH AN ACCOUNT OF THE LIFE OF
THE CELEBRATED ARTIST, F. B. CARPENTER, AUTHOR
OF THE GREAT NATIONAL PAINTING,

THE FIRST READING

OF THE

EMANCIPATION PROCLAMATION

BEFORE THE CABINET BY PRESIDENT LINCOLN;

INCLUDING ALSO

AN ACCOUNT OF THE PICTURE; AN ACCOUNT OF THE CRISIS WHICH PRO-
DUCED IT; AND AN APPENDIX CONTAINING THE GREAT PROCLAMA-
TION AND THE SUPPLEMENTARY PROCLAMATION OF JAN-
UARY 1, 1863; TOGETHER WITH A PORTRAIT OF THE
ARTIST, AND A KEY TO THE PICTURE.

COMPILED BY

FRED. B. PERKINS,

EDITOR OF "THE GALAXY," FORMERLY ONE OF THE EDITORS OF THE NEW
YORK "TRIBUNE," AND OF THE NEW YORK "INDEPENDENT."

Published by
A. J. JOHNSON, NEW YORK.
F. G. & A. C. ROWE, CLEVELAND, OHIO.
C. ALLEN, M.D., CHICAGO, ILL.
1867.

ENTERED, ACCORDING TO ACT OF CONGRESS, IN THE YEAR 1867, BY

A. J. JOHNSON,

IN THE CLERK'S OFFICE OF THE DISTRICT COURT OF THE UNITED STATES
FOR THE SOUTHERN DISTRICT OF NEW YORK.

DAVIES & KENT,
Electrotypers and Stereotypers,
183 WILLIAM ST., N. Y.

PREFACE.

THIS rapidly-written little book is intended to serve as a companion and key to Mr. Carpenter's great picture. The sketches of the persons whom that picture represents, the account of the picture itself, of the crisis which suggested it, and of the painter who executed it, are all meant to give such information as will help to a clearer and fuller understanding of the painting.

The writer has no wish to conceal the fact that he is what is called an "extreme Radical;" but he has sought to omit himself from this subject, and to sketch the persons here represented, not with reference to any approval or disapproval of his own, but as they may justly be believed to have meant while laboring honestly to the best of their ability for the preservation of the Union.

The principal authorities used in the work, besides some standard books of reference accessible to all, are : Mr. Carpenter's own very interesting work, " Six Months at the White House," a singularly full collection of the most graphic and entertaining anecdotes and reminiscences ; the lives of Mr. Lincoln by Raymond, Holland, Barrett, Crosby, and Mrs. Hanaford ; Trowbridge's biography of Mr. Chase, entitled " Ferry Boy and Financier ;" and Baker's Life of Seward.

Technical criticism of Mr. Carpenter's picture has been avoided ; as the writer is one of the very few persons living who do not understand the business of art criticism.

FRED. B. PERKINS.

January 2d, 1867.

TABLE OF CONTENTS.

THE PICTURE AND THE MEN.

I.

F. B. CARPENTER.

FRANCIS BICKNELL CARPENTER, painter of the picture of "The First Reading of the Emancipation Proclamation by President Lincoln to his Cabinet," is an artist of high reputation, having already painted portraits of Ex-President Tyler, President Pierce, President Fillmore, Chief-Justice Chase, Secretary Marcy, Secretary Seward, Senators Cass and Houston, Attorney-General Cushing, and many other eminent persons besides. Like Mr. Lincoln, Mr. Fillmore, and many more of the distinguished Americans who have sat to him, Mr. Carpenter was born in humble circumstances, and has earned his own prosperity and reputation by good conduct and hard work—a truly American career.

Mr. Carpenter was born in Homer, Cortland County, New York, Aug. 6, 1830. His father was a respectable farmer, of almost as practical a character as King George the Second, whose whole doctrine about the fine arts was expressed by his saying, in his German brogue, "I hate *bainting*, and *boetry* too." Young

Carpenter was intended by his good father for a farmer, or perhaps a country merchant, and like other country boys he was sent to the "deestrick school," or American university.

As soon as the boy was old enough to have any preferences, he showed a strong love for Art. This was when he was at school, and eight years old, and its first occasion was his seeing and admiring a clever pencil-drawing made on a panel of the school-room door, one day at recess, by a schoolmate named Otis, subsequently a distinguished physician in New York. This door-panel picture stirred up in young Carpenter the desire and resolve which made him an artist. For the next five or six years the little fellow worked away with untiring industry, drawing pictures of all sorts of things, on whatever would hold a picture. He had neither instruction, books, nor models. Farmers' sons seldom have much money, and the resolute boy often traveled three miles to the village to invest his total capital, usually not over two cents, in a sheet of unruled foolscap and a pencil. Blank leaves out of old account books, all manner·of blank and waste papers, blank walls, both inside of the house and out, smooth pieces of board—every available surface—were industriously used instead of canvas, and some of these monuments of youthful effort still decorate the walls of the old homestead. As in many other cases, this youthful period was one of ambition as great as its experience was small; the boy soared promptly into the ideal realm of historical painting, and among other scenes chalked on the side of the old barn the capture of André, and William Tell Shooting the Apple from his Son's Head.

All this vigorous industry met with little response, except snubs and sneers. Mr. Carpenter promptly rebuked every hint from his son about becoming a painter. And Deacon I——, one of the more eminent dignitaries of the neighborhood, when somebody asked him some question about all this drawing, answered, with great scorn, "Humph! you can't turn over a chip on his father's farm without findin' a pictur' of a chicken or sunthin' on t'other side on't!" And this, by the way, is all that is known of the eminent and influential deacon.

When young Carpenter was thirteen, his father sought to put him in the way of earning a respectable living, and secured for him, to this end, employment in a grocery store in Ithaca. But drawing molasses was not the kind of drawing which the young gentleman preferred, and the worthy man of codfish soon became sure that the youth was "a poor creature." For six months he tried faithfully to make the boy do something useful, but all in vain; and quite discouraged, he sent him home to his father with a letter saying that he showed nothing of the intelligence necessary for mercantile business, and that his mind turned entirely to drawing and reading. Therefore, advised the good grocer, the best thing to be done with him is to keep him at work on the farm! This sage advice was followed, and doubtless Mr. Carpenter, senior, and the other elders, concluded, as Sir Isaac Newton's teacher did about him, that the boy was a hopeless dunce.

Just at this time Mr. George L. Clough, a young artist from Auburn, N. Y., came to Homer to paint some portraits, and young Carpenter, getting permission to see him work, watched the operation of painting for the first time in his life, and with the keenness of a famished man's appetite. Some new ideas on the subject of color were thus acquired, and with the prompt executive impulse of a natural worker, the boy quickly set himself to try them. Colors and pencils he had not, and could not buy, and the suggestion of a neighbor that house paint would do nicely to begin with, was a welcome one. Away he went to the village and got one pound of white lead; back again home, and there he found some lampblack which was used to mark sheep. This served for light and shade; and for color, he discovered some lumps of Venetian red, which had dried up in a corner of the barn until so hard that he had to pound them up on the door-step. His pencils were of the sort used by carriage-painters, his pallet was whittled out of a piece of shingle, and his canvas a piece of coat lining. Thus armed, the youthful artist coaxed his mother to sit, and soon outlined and almost completed an easily recognized likeness, with what curious grays, reds, and browns it is not easy to imagine. But all parties to this great work were afraid of Mr. Carpenter, senior, who had grown really angry in opposing the "nonsense," as he termed it, of his son; and so it was kept a profound secret. Now Master Frank had become rather unpleasantly conspicuous on the farm for being always invisible at work-hours; he was always out of the way—"'round the corner," like Mr. Chevy Slyme in the novel. One day the impatient father wanted Frank's help, and so, instead of calling him, went right to his room. Striding angrily in, he saw the picture, and stopped short:

"Who is that?" he asked.

"Don't you know, father?" said the boy, roguishly, and yet earnestly.

"It is your mother, I suppose," said the father, gruffly, though honestly; and he was somewhat conscience-struck at seeing that the boy who had not mind enough for groceries could actually make a likeness. He turned and hastily left the room without a word, but his manner toward his son at once became much more agreeable. Indeed, he even sat to him himself, selecting only rainy days, when he could not work, and feeling so slight an interest in the matter that he fell asleep on one occasion at least, within ten minutes after sitting down. Nevertheless, the likeness was unmistakable, though rough; and the neighbors said it was decidedly better than the works of the wandering artists who had been the only painters there before. A small compliment, yet doubtless true.

At length the sturdy opposition of the father to the single ambition of the son gave way, and it was agreed that young Carpenter might obtain some regular professional instruction. Promptly and joyfully the boy applied to Mr. Sandford Thayer, of Syracuse, who examined him closely, received him into his studio, and during five months gave him a course of judicious instruction which became a solid foundation for subsequent technical acquirements. Mr. Thayer had been a student under the eminent portrait-painter Elliott, who visited Syracuse and painted several portraits in Mr. Thayer's studio while young Carpenter was there.

Mr. Elliott, a genial and thoroughly kind-hearted man, took a great interest in the zealous young apprentice, allowed him full opportunity of observing his methods, gave him advice which was of much service to him, and has ever since been his steadfast friend.

Mr. Carpenter opened a studio for the first time, in his native village of Homer, in the year 1846, before he was sixteen. He boarded at home for a few weeks, but his father soon notified him that, having chosen his profession, he must live entirely by it; so he stoutly went into the village and electioneered for board from house to house, offering to paint portraits in pay for his meals. For the first year or two his "chariot-wheels drave heavily" enough. His first commission was to paint the portrait of a clerk in the village store, who paid him with cloth enough for a pair of panta-loons; and his second brought him a pair of boots. But this success, though not very brilliant, was exceed-ingly substantial, and it was real practice, too; so the youth worked on with good courage. His first large cash fee was ten dollars. This sum was paid him by Hon. H. S. Randall, who lived in the vicinity, for drawings to illustrate his well-known book on sheep husbandry. Mr. Randall, recognizing the talent of the young artist, soon afterward employed him to paint his portrait. Shortly afterward, he painted the por-traits of the nine survivors of the original Trustees of Cortland Academy; and the pictures, still adorning the Academy library, though crude and rough, possess all the chief characteristics of the artist's style. In 1848, Mr. Carpenter sent to the "American Art Union," then a flourishing institution in New York city, an ideal female head. This was submitted to the purchasing committee along with about four hundred other paintings, and was one of the twelve which they decided to buy, out of the whole number; and the struggling young countryman received what was to him the really handsome sum of fifty dollars. This was a genuine artistic and financial success, and was the beginning of Mr. Carpenter's career of efficient professional labor · and prosperity, though he had poverty and difficulty yet to encounter. The Art Union afterward bought several others of Mr. Carpenter's pictures, being all that he offered them; and he now had a good many commissions for portraits, though at low rates.

In the spring of 1851 Mr. Carpenter established himself in New York city, sending to the Exhibition of the Academy of Design a portrait of a young girl, which was liked by many, and so much so by W. S. Mount, the painter, that he took pains to become acquainted with Mr. Carpenter, sat to him, and did all in his power to make him known. In the next autumn Mr. Carpenter married Miss Augusta H. Prentiss.

The following winter he executed a full-length portrait of Mr. David Leavitt, which, at the next Exhibition of the Academy, was very highly praised, and the artist was now chosen Associate of the Academy, at what was then an unusually early age. In the autumn of 1852, Hon. D. A. Bokee, of Brooklyn, commissioned Mr. Carpenter to paint a full-length of President Fillmore, which was a very successful picture, and received an extremely flattering testimonial in a letter from the President. The city of New York bought a duplicate of this picture. During the first winter of

Gen. Pierce's term, Mr. Carpenter was employed to paint his picture, the President consenting only with great reluctance, because several previous pictures had all been unsatisfactory. He, however, quickly found himself much interested in the work, and both he and his friends considered it beyond comparison the best portrait ever taken of him. At the urgent request of Mr. and Mrs. Pierce, Mr. Carpenter afterward executed successfully the difficult task of painting a picture of their deceased son, the materials being only a defective daguerreotype, and the recollections of surviving friends. The genial personal qualities of the artist, and his peculiar professional abilities, had by this time secured him efficient friends at Washington; and in the beginning of 1855 he went to Washington again, commissioned to paint Governor Marcy, and Senators Cass, Chase, Houston, and Seward. Congress adjourned before the work was completed, but President Pierce invited the artist to stay at the White House for the rest of his visit, and here he executed two portraits of Gov. Marcy, one of Attorney-General Cushing, and a profile head of the President.

Among the other portraits painted by Mr. Carpenter may be mentioned those of Henry Ward Beecher, his father, Rev. Lyman Beecher, Rev. R. S. Storrs, ex-Mayors Talmadge, Brush, Lambert, and Hall of Brooklyn, General McDonald, Professors Gibbs and Aiken, General Fremont, Rev. Drs. Cox, Field, Bushnell, and Bacon, Captain Hudson of the first telegraph fleet, etc., etc.

Mr. Carpenter is now comfortably established in New York city, and is enjoying the reputation and income which are the just earnings of so much undiscouraged toil and sincere thought and effort.

Mr. Carpenter is distinctly a portrait-painter, both by natural preference and natural endowment. From the very first awakening of his inclination for Art, his attention was always drawn most keenly to the human face and head. These he studies with instinctive special love; enjoys their traits and their meaning, and labors with his happiest spontaneous thoughts and skill to reproduce them on canvas.

This natural preference, however, would be very imperfect without that fitness for the work which Mr. Carpenter's mental and physical constitution affords. He has a quick and sensitive intuition of character, ready sympathies, a calm and even cheerfulness of disposition, is perfectly unassuming in fact and in manner, and is at once kindly, receptive, and appreciative. The student of character will easily see that these traits constitute the agreeable companion as well as the intelligent painter. This is just the combination calculated to render Mr. Carpenter a welcome friend to the numerous eminent political leaders whom he has painted. They are quick-witted and clear-headed men, and have a pretty good judgment on the essential merits of a picture; they spend their lives in contending with rivals and opponents; and they find in the artist a painter just and competent without flattery, a friend, calm and appreciative and genial, who wants neither influence nor office, and whose easy conversation and pleasant society make his sitter's chair a sort of rest and home. Mr. Fillmore was once asked by a lady if his sittings to Mr. Carpenter were not tedious ? " O no, madam," he replied, promptly; " it is the pleasantest hour in the day."

Criticisms already printed have recognized more or less clearly the peculiar traits above stated. Thus the *Home Journal*, in 1856, in speaking of Mr. Carpenter's works in the Exhibition of that year, observed: " The painter of these pictures is perhaps the most variously self-adaptable, the most symmetrically constituted, safe, and sure, of any of our portrait-painters. If he can be characterized by anything, it is the almost unexampled number of his variations of color and style, to suit the complexion and character of his sitters." And the N. Y. *Evening Post* subsequently remarked: "The portraits by this artist are remarkable chiefly for their subtile mentality; for their faithful rendering of the inward life and disposition."

Mr. Carpenter's character as a man may be in some measure estimated by his career as an artist. He possesses excellent mental and moral endowments, being resolute, industrious, prompt, orderly, and efficient in executive matters, and upright and blameless in all the relations of a man and a citizen. During the first ten months of his residence in New York he had but one or two commissions for portraits; but he did not by any means sit idle for that. One of his earliest resolves was, to keep at work at something; and if he had no paying sitters, he would prevail on friends or acquaintances to sit, executing their pictures with as much conscientious study and effort as if they had every one been Presidents. This was sound business practice as well as sound Art practice, because his skill increased just as much as if his time were full; and when the next commission did come, he was sure to paint better than ever before. Nor has he grown idle yet. The true ideal of the artist's industry is exactly, in Art, what the Christian's contest is in life: to labor all his life toward a perfection which he is bound to work for just as hard as if he could reach it. The eminent English painter Mulready became, in 1817, one of the instructors or "visitors" in the "life school," or place for learning how to draw the human figure. In 1863, after holding this position for forty-six years, the old man declared— "I have, from the first moment I became a visitor in the life school, drawn there *as if I were drawing for a prize.*" He was, too; but it was a higher prize than any Academy could give. Sir Charles Eastlake said that Mr. Mulready was "the best and most judicious teacher the Royal Academy ever had;" and Charles Landseer said, "Perhaps neither is there now, nor at any time has there been, so great a draughtsman as Mr. Mulready." Mr. Carpenter is not yet the first painter in the world, but then he is not so old as Mulready, who was born in 1786. But his industry is as thorough in principle as that of the veteran painter; it was only the other day that he showed a friend "Chapman's American Drawing Book," which he had under his arm, stating that he had purchased it with the intention of studying it thoroughly.

Mr. Carpenter's views of the ethics of Art, as well as his moral and religious sentiments generally, have always been ideally high. In youth, he conceived that the artist ought of necessity to be of the purest character, and with boyish enthusiasm he resolved to endeavor to realize in himself in some measure the union

of artistic ability and moral excellence. The endeavor
has consistently been made. The very endeavor enno-
bles. It is the seeker himself after such high endowments who most deeply feels the weakness of human
efforts after goodness. But the high position and the
spotless name which Mr. Carpenter has gained are
most fully believed his just due by those who know
him best.

He is a man of wide intelligence and considerable
literary ability and attainment outside of his profession, and his book, " Six Months at the White House,"
giving the history of his stay there while at work on
his great picture, is a singularly interesting one. Mr.
Carpenter is of middle height, rather slender, with del-
licate features, abundant straight black hair, and dark
gray eyes. His voice is rather low and of agreeable
tone; and in manner he is extremely quiet, meditative,
and often apparently quite absorbed in reflection or
revery, seeming to receive impressions from persons and
things around him unconsciously, rather than by keeping
his intellect at work to seize them; in short, he is a
gentleman, and those who know him best love him most.

II.

THE OCCASION.

THE Emancipation of the Slaves in the United States belongs to a class of events so lofty and so vast in nature and meaning, that it is an effort to comprehend them. It has often been said that no single deed so great has been done on earth since Christ was crucified. If any can be compared with it, they are the very greatest: the Christianizing of the Roman Empire by Constantine; the issue of Magna Charta to England; the inauguration of the Reformation by Luther; the Declaration of Independence. Indeed, it would be easy to show that it is linked with these in one chain of cause and effect. The last three of the series are obviously so related. The Declaration of Independence was the logical result of the principles of Luther put in practice by English Puritans, and announced in their political applications by the descendants and successors of those Puritans, the Continental Congress. Emancipation has made the United States the banner-bearer of mankind—the foremost nation in human progress—just as the Declaration did in 1776.

The train of circumstances that preceded President Lincoln's Proclamation of September 22, 1862, is, of course, of great historical interest and importance. The Constitution of the United States was in its very framing put together with compromises about Slavery.

The first period of the history of this subject comes down to about the end of the last century. During that period there was much opposition to slaveholding, by men of high moral nature and profound political insight, all over the country, and since business interest coincided with the moral duty of the case, there was decidedly a tendency toward a gradual dying out of the system.

The second period begins with that great increase in the production of cotton which resulted from the invention and use of Whitney's cotton-gin, dating from about 1793. This increase caused slaves to grow rapidly more valuable, and it is a matter of course that men desire to think, and therefore tend strongly to think, that what is very profitable must be right, or at least excusable.

The third period may be reckoned from the beginning of the abolition movement of Mr. Garrison and his associates down to the date of the Proclamation, in which it culminated. The first period was that of feeble moral reprobation of slavery; the second, that of increasing financial acquiescence in slavery; the third, that of earnest moral attack and defense of slavery, the financial and political aspects of it not being now the really predominant ones.

In this third period came the successive excitements of the Missouri Compromise, the "incendiary document" and "gag-law" time, the "Political Abolition" time, the "Free Soil" time, the "Kansas" time, the "John Brown" time, and lastly the rebellion.

The rebellion was the effort of the slave interest to take a snap judgment, so to speak, on a question which the country was evidently in a steady advance toward deciding on the side of freedom. And so much organization and preparation had the South, so utterly ignorant of the scheme was the North, so strong was the combination of a united South, Northern sympathizers, and European monarchies, and so undecided and dormant were the convictions of very many even of the loyal Northern men, that undoubtedly the nation had a narrow escape from destruction, winning in the conflict not merely nor even chiefly as the richest and strongest of the two warring powers, but by means of the strength of the patriotism and moral convictions that germinated and grew vigorously and fast by the stimulus of the very fire that was kindled to consume them.

The words in which Mr. Lincoln described the occasion on which the Proclamation was planned and issued have all his striking and characteristic plainness, simplicity, directness, and graphic force. He said to Mr. Carpenter, "Things had gone on from bad to worse, until I felt that we had reached the end of our rope on the plan of operations we had been pursuing; that we had about played our last card, and must change our tactics, or lose the game."

This time was the latter part of the summer of 1862, the period of the discouragement produced by the "Peninsular campaign." It is true that Union successes had taken place at several points upon the outer circumference of the rebellion; but its main body yet remained substantially untouched, and above all, its mailed head—consisting of the main army under Lee, protected by the strong and extremely defensible coun-

try of Northern Virginia—that mailed head which it
constantly thrust out at Washington and the North,
was still full of threatening and dangerous life. Although the Government had in the field in the beginning of that year more than 660,000 soldiers, and a navy
of 246 ships, 22,000 men, and 1,892 guns, no decisive
injury had yet been done to the enemy. Political
opponents at home were raising an awful clamor about
the inefficiency and incapacity of the Administration,
and a good many even of its friends were joining in
the cry. There was a very visible and growing weariness among the people, of conscriptions, of taxes, of
the disordered currency, of the increasing prices of all
sorts of manufactured and imported commodities. Mr.
Greeley even goes so far as to say that it is doubtful
whether a popular vote on giving up the fight, if taken
during the year next after the issue of the Proclamation, would not have been affirmative. This opinion,
however, is probably shaded by its author's well-known
liability to look on the dark side, for the patriotism
of Mr. Greeley can not be doubted.

However, Mr. Blair urged to Mr. Lincoln as a reason
against the Proclamation, that its issue would cause
the loss of the fall elections; and, sure enough, it apparently did. In ten States which gave Mr. Lincoln in
1860 more than 208,000 majority, the Administration
candidates for State offices were beaten in the fall of
1862 by nearly 36,000. This, however, was rather the
result of the hesitating non-emancipation policy of the
previous two years, and its attendant ill success, than the
result of the new emancipation policy, only just announced, and not yet proved as an influence in the war.

It was the result of the old mistakes, not of the new correction. As soon as the new policy was well understood, and began to show its operation, there was no more fear of losing elections by it. It became the policy of the nation, and ceased to be a party question, just as the support of the Government had ceased to be a party question ever since Sumter was attacked.

Assuredly the people of the United States waited long enough before resolving upon universal freedom. Most undoubtedly the Proclamation was made at the right time to take the great mass of the nation with it. Any time would have been too late for extremists on one side, and too early for extremists on the other. But the deeds of Mr. Lincoln were the resolutions of the loyal people as a whole, and his course was with a sort of magnetic truth what they felt to be best.

It was therefore really the people who did the acts which the President superintended, as their chief manager. Even after the war broke out, it took nearly two years to bring the people into the conviction that emancipation must come—that this vast moral justice was absolutely indispensable, alike to free the North from its false position and to put the South · in its true one—to unite and strengthen the right side and to cripple the wrong. Accordingly, the war had commenced with the most circumspect and systematic observance of "conservative" precedent in this matter, and went on for a long time in a manner which, so far as slavery was concerned, "could not offend the feelings of the most fastidious" slaveholder. So cautious and conservative a statesman as Edward Everett asserted that it was matter of grave doubt " whether

any act of the Government of the United States was
necessary to liberate the slaves in a State which is in
open rebellion." Prophetic minds felt from the very
first gun that the day of universal freedom was at
hand. But prophetic minds are few; national convictions and sentiments change very gradually; and
before emancipation could be safely made the law, an
underpinning of public opinion had to be slowly laid
for it, even though thousands of millions of dollars
were expended in the building, and though the structure was cemented and soaked in the blood of our
bravest men. In the United States, no law will ope-
rate which public opinion does not support. This is
true, no matter whether such law be right or wrong,
It is a fundamental fact in democracies. It has been
proved over and over in laws on the liquor question,
and perhaps an understanding of this may have influ-
enced the President's delay in the matter. However
that may be, Mr. Lincoln, while personally profoundly
anxious for universal freedom, was utterly immovable
in the resolution to maintain the national existence
within undoubted constitutional forms if possible—and
persisted in this course, until, as he said, its last card
had been played. This is most strongly shown in his
letter to Mr. Greeley of Aug. 22, 1862, a remarkably
terse and forcible statement in every possible variation
of assertion, of this object. "My paramount object," he
said, "is to save the Union, and not either to save or
to destroy slavery. If I could save the Union without
freeing any slaves, I would do it—if I could save it by
freeing all the slaves, I would do it—and if I could do
it by freeing some and leaving others alone, I would also

do that." Mr. Seward took it for granted that the war would not touch the slavery question at all. In his dispatch to Minister Dayton, of April 22d, 1861, he said, with mistaken prediction, "The condition of slavery in the several States will remain just the same, whether it (the rebellion) succeed or fail." The manifesto of Gen. McDowell on his first entry into Virginia, in July, 1861, contained nothing that showed whether or not such a thing as slavery existed. McClellan's proclamation in West Virginia of May 26, 1861, had before announced that he would "subdue slave insurrection with an iron hand." Gen. T. W. Sherman, after the victory at Port Royal, expressly disclaimed any intention of meddling with slavery. Gen. Dix, in occupying the Eastern Shore counties of Virginia, did the like, and shut his lines to fugitives from slavery; Gen. Halleck, on succeeding Fremont in Missouri, did the like, and, moreover, expelled from the protection of his lines such fugitives as had already taken refuge there. Gen. Burnside published a similar disclaimer on occupying Roanoke Island; Gen. Buell in Tennessee and Kentucky, Gen. Hooker on the upper Potomac, Gen. Williams in Louisiana, did the like, and still further, they opened their camps to slave-catchers, and officially helped them, by ordering the surrender of fugitives, and even by furnishing detachments or details to assist in the chase. Fremont's proclamation of freedom in Missouri was at once modified within the statutory limits; Hunter's in South Carolina was promptly annulled; Phelps' at Ship Island would have been, had not circumstances rendered it unnecessary. Never since the creation of the world was there seen

any war before, conducted by the year together, on the
avowed principle and in the diligent and effective practice of not touching the greatest source of the enemy's
strength, of assuring him the full enjoyment of it, of
carefully returning to him any of it that got away, and
of helping him chase it right through the very ranks of
the extra-magnanimous belligerents. It was exerting our
whole force to protect the enemy's powder-magazine.

Even when the course of events gradually forced the
nation from this strange method of making war by
guaranteeing the enemy, the change was made very
slowly and gradually. Officers commanding in one
and another locality found it a physical impossibility
to dispense with the services of the negroes, and a
moral impossibility to treat them otherwise than as
men and freemen. Such cases multiplied in number
and grew in importance for months and months, and a
series of partial measures, dealing with slavery in the
District of Columbia, or with slaves as contraband of
war, or as subject to confiscation, or as fit material for
enlistment, had successively tested the public sentiment
of the country for a long time before the cautious
President could determine that the hour was come for
proclaiming "liberty throughout all the land." At
last, however, it was time. With true instinct, the
man of the people felt that the will of the people was
ripe for the new policy. The furious battles of South
Mountain and Antietam, and the subsequent retreat of
Lee, beaten and driven over the Potomac from his first
invasion of Maryland, constituted a turn in the tide of
affairs which enabled the Proclamation to appear in
victory instead of defeat.

As prompt at snatching an occasion as he was slow in maturing the purpose to be served, Mr. Lincoln instantly published the grandest utterance of the age. It was not, it is true, an unconditional assertion either of the rights of man, or of the freedom of any class of men. In fact, as it was worded, it gave the rebels an opportunity of retaining the system of slavery in every Southern State; for it was not in itself a gift of emancipation, but only contingent notice of emancipation at one hundred days. Mr. Lincoln had no wish to seem to do a great action himself, nor to put forth any impressive phrases. It is a feature most characteristic of his simple, weighty, honest, unconscious, straightforward nature, that in this great state paper, announcing a radical change in the social and political policy of the strongest nation in the world, relieving the foremost people on earth from a social blot and blunder which would have disgraced and hampered the hindmost, admitting four millions of chattels personal into the brotherhood of man, and completing for the first time the exemplification of Christian morals in the legal action of a democracy—that in doing all this, he so did it as to seem not to do it; as to allow it to happen, not at once, by the force of an actual fiat, but after three months, in the form of the obligatory fulfillment of a past promise; and even then, not by any act of his, or even of the nation, but simply by the neglect of the persons addressed to perform the plainest duties of the citizen. For the reader of the Proclamation will see at once how entirely it throws the responsibility of the act upon the South. If the Southern States had discontinued their rebellious organization and resumed

their places in Congress within the hundred days, the
nation would have been bound to accept such action
and appearance as a reparation in full, and to have
suffered the whole fabric of slavery to remain as before,
not merely upheld by the laws of each State and the
entire frame of Southern society, but, as before the
war, by the acquiescence and moral support of the
whole United States. Doubtless, Mr. Lincoln may
have felt that there was in fact no danger of such submission and return ; but the absolute disinterestedness,
profound caution, sagacious foreseeing statesmanship,
and lawyer-like clearness, accuracy, and safety of the
drafting of the paper are none the less wonderful for
that. The Proclamation does not say one word nor do
one thing not absolutely necessary ; it neither discusses
a principle, nor argues a case, nor expresses a feeling.
It does not even put forth its real and vast significance
directly ; much less with ornaments of speech or largeness of words. It is the barest, briefest notice to legal
delinquents to return to duty, with a proviso of further
action if they do not return. It is so arranged, that if
there be a chance not to secure emancipation, the
chance shall be taken ; that if the crowning glory of
the century can be avoided, it shall be avoided ; that
if the signer can escape the credit of freeing four millions of slaves, he shall escape it ; that if the South can
be induced to retain their labor system, they shall retain it ; that if the actual responsibility of freedom is to
rest anywhere, it shall rest upon the rebel slaveholders
themselves. It embodies the utter abnegation of personal merit or emotion ; the entire avoidance of controversy upon either any principle in doctrine or any

material interest or association of human beings; it is the simple, plain statement of one future fact, unless there shall happen another future fact. And notwithstanding all this guarded negation of statement and conditional assertion, yet such were the aspects of the war in the field, and of the public opinion of the North, that these two gigantic forces, embodying the moral sum total of the United States for the time being, inspired into the words of this plain short paper that whole and complete and immense meaning which has rendered it immortal.

30

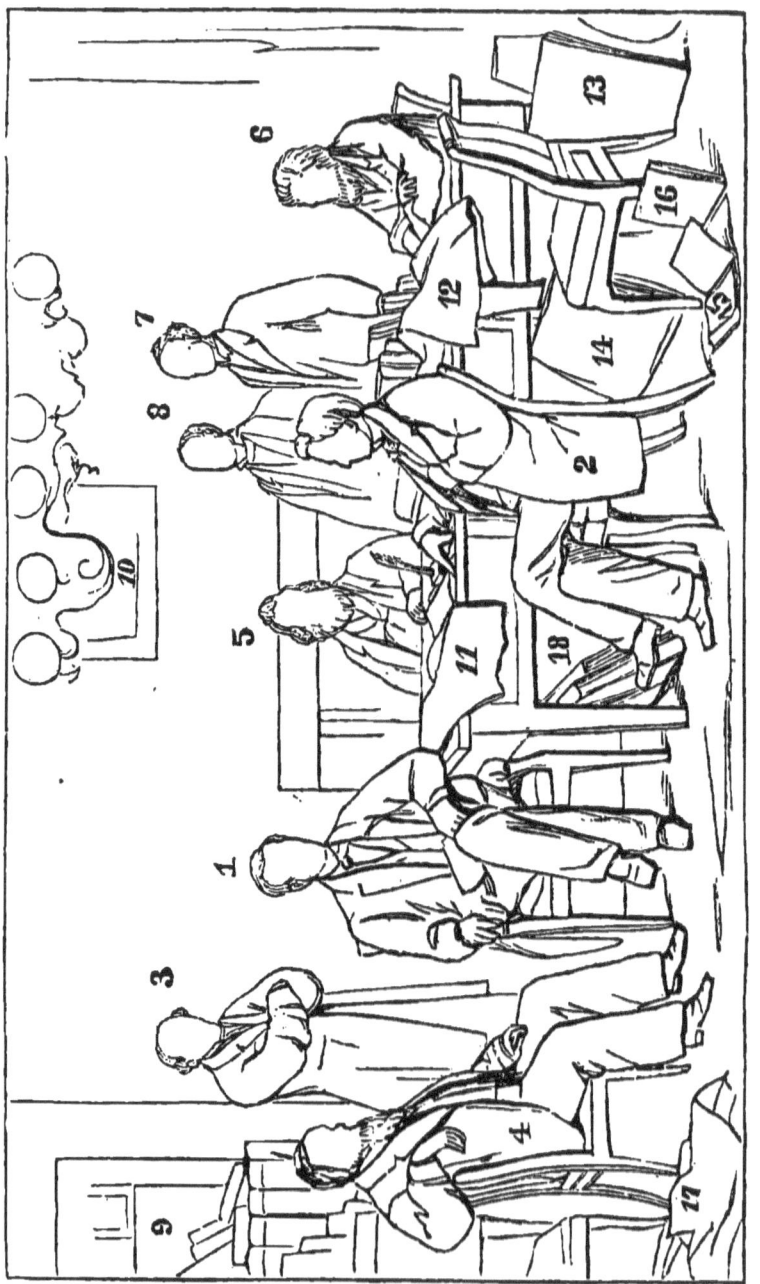

THE KEY TO THE PICTURE.

THE MEN.

1. PRESIDENT LINCOLN.
2. WILLIAM H. SEWARD, Secretary of State.
3. SALMON P. CHASE, Secretary of Treasury.
4. EDWIN M. STANTON, Secretary of War.
5. GIDEON WELLES, Secretary of Navy.
6. EDWARD BATES, Attorney-General.
7. MONTGOMERY BLAIR, Postmaster-General.
8. CALEB B. SMITH, Secretary of Interior.

☞ The room is the Official Chamber of the White House, in which all Cabinet meetings are held, and in which the President receives calls upon official business.

ACCESSORIES.

9. Photograph of Simon Cameron, Ex-Sec. War.
10. Portrait of Andrew Jackson.
11. Parchment Copy of the Constitution.
12. Map of Seat of War in Virginia.
13. Map showing Slave Population in graduated light and shade.
14. War Department Portfolio.
15. Story's "Commentaries on the Constitution."
16. Whiting's "War Powers of the President."
17. New York *Tribune.*
18. Two volumes *Congressional Globe.*

III.

THE PICTURE.

The original conception of Mr. Carpenter's great picture is due to his profound loyalty to the United States, his fervent devotion to Freedom, his deep exultation when the issue of the Great Proclamation announced that Slavery was Abolished, his strong desire to execute some work within the field of his art which should express his appreciation of the questions of the war, and the nation's action upon them, and his honorable ambition to associate his own name and reputation with an occasion so glorious. The artist thus describes his own first clear conception of the time and sentiment of his picture, in his "Six Months at the White House :"

"The long-prayed-for year of jubilee had come; the bonds of the oppressed were loosed; the prison doors were opened. 'Behold,' said a voice, 'how a man may be exalted to a dignity and glory almost divine, and give freedom to a race! Surely Art should unite with Eloquence and Poetry to celebrate such a theme.' I conceived of that band of men upon whom the eyes of the world centred as never before upon ministers of state, gathered in council, depressed, perhaps disheartened at the vain efforts of many months to restore the supremacy of the Government. I saw, in thought, the head of the nation, bowed down with his weight of care and responsibility, solemnly announcing, as he unfolded the prepared draft of the Proclamation, that the time for the inauguration of this policy had arrived ; I endeavored to imagine the conflicting emotions of satisfaction, doubt, and distrust with which such an announcement would be received by men of the varied characteristics of the assembled councilors."

This was in the end of the year 1863, the first day of which had witnessed the issuing of the Supplementary Proclamation announcing the fulfillment of the promise. For some weeks the painter, after his manner, brooded silently over his design. Gradually the group assumed in his imagination such a form and arrangement as satisfied his conception of what the assembly must have been. Mr. Carpenter is not without a decided tendency toward those lofty realms of human aspiration and emotional thought, the mystical and the supernatural ; and he records a coincidence in the matter of adjusting his design which is sufficiently striking. "In seeking a point of unity or action for the picture," he says, "I was impressed with the conviction that important modifications followed the reading of the Proclamation at the suggestion of the Secretary of State, and I determined upon such an incident as the moment of time to be represented. I was subsequently surprised and gratified when Mr. Lincoln himself, reciting the history of the Proclamation to me, dwelt particularly upon the fact, that not only was the time of its issue decided by Secretary Seward's advice, but that one of the most important words in the document was added through his strenuous representations." •

The design thus determined, it remained to execute
it, and Mr. Carpenter first consulted Mr. Samuel Sinclair, now publisher of the N. Y. *Tribune*, upon the
means of interesting in the scheme Messrs. Schuyler
Colfax and Owen Lovejoy, who should, in their turn,
influence their personal and political friend the President. This shrewd little piece of wire-pulling succeeded, for Mr. Sinclair, being the very next week in Washington, went with Mr. Colfax to Mr. Lincoln, explained
the plan, and without much difficulty obtained his assent.

The road was now clear for the execution of the am-
bitious scheme of the artist; but how was he to travel
in it? " Who goeth a warfare any time at his own
charges ?"—and besides, he had not the means for such
unscriptural expenditure, even were he so anti-biblical
as to make it. A second coincidence attended the
solution of the difficulty. He left home one morning,
pondering deeply upon the financial lion in his path;
and contriving and rejecting, with increasing discouragement, one expedient after another, he reached the
door of the building where his studio was established,
and was about to enter. At that moment he happened
to observe a gentleman who was intently examining
some pictures in a shop window. Something familiar
in the air of the figure attracted the artist, and when
in a few moments the gazer turned round, it proved to
be Frederick A. Lane, Esq., an old acquaintance who,
five years before, had lived near Mr. Carpenter in
Brooklyn, and, like him, had at that time been struggling hard for a living, though in the dry path of law,
instead of the supposed more flowery ways of Art.

Mr. Carpenter asked Mr. Lane up into his studio,

and there was some comparing of old reminiscences
and late experiences. The lawyer had prospered in
business and in purse; the artist was still poor. Suddenly the sensitive painter was stirred with the thought
that this meeting was "providential." A less spontaneous man would have reckoned this a mere conceit,
and would have reasoned away from it. But the mental constitution of an artist has often much of the same
quickness of intuition and instinctive reliance upon it,
which is usually attributed to women. Mr. Carpenter at once briefly laid before his visitor his whole
scheme. Mr. Lane quietly heard him through. "Are
you sure of Mr. Lincoln's consent and co-operation?"
he asked. The painter told him of the promise which
Messrs. Sinclair and Colfax had received. "Then," said
this liberal friend, "you shall paint the picture. Take
plenty of time. Make it the great work of your life;
and draw upon me for whatever funds you will require
to the end."

On the 4th of February, 1864, Mr. Carpenter went
to Washington, and calling next day upon Hon. Owen
Lovejoy, obtained a note of introduction to Mr. Lincoln.
After waiting in vain for two days for an opportunity
to present it, the artist at last went up to the White
House on the afternoon of Saturday, and taking his
place in what the French call the "tail" of citizens who
were filing past the patient President, each shaking
hands and uttering some observation as they went,
like so many customers popping their letters into some
crowded post-office window, he took his turn, and was
named to Mr. Lincoln. After a moment's recollection,
Mr. Lincoln said, "O yes, I know—this is the painter;"

and standing up as tall as he could—which was much
—he added, with a queer look, " Do you think, Mr.
Carpenter, that you can make a handsome picture of
me ?" The painter was taken aback at this very direct
query, and too polite to say No, and too honest to say
Yes, he answered at random, coming, however, enough
to the point to ask if he could have a private interview
after the reception. "I reckon!" was the reply of the
Executive, as he went gravely on again with his pump-
handling.

When this tiresome ceremony was over, the painter
was admitted to the President's office, where Mr. Lincoln was already hard at work signing acts of Congress. He gave his visitor a seat, and received and read
Mr. Lovejoy's note of introduction. Then, taking off his
spectacles, he turned to the artist and said, in his characteristic way, " Well, Mr. Carpenter, we will *turn you
in loose* here"—as if the painter were a harmless sort
of beast, safe in pasture without " poke" or "hobbling"
—"and try to give you a good chance to work out
your idea." It is curious to consider how many of the
rulers of the earth would have thus assented to an
artist's proposal for a great historical picture of one of
the turning-points in human progress, in a sentence of
twenty-one words (not counting the name of the person spoken to), all monosyllables but one, and expressing their thought with a metaphor accurate, forcible,
and taken from the pasture and the oxen.

The enthusiastic artist began to express as well as
he could, one or another lofty idea of his intended
work. The President paid little attention to this, but
after his fashion went straight to the root of the matter

and proceeded to give his auditor a history of the circumstances. We transcribe Mr. Lincoln's own words as given by Mr. Carpenter.*

"It had got to be midsummer, 1862. Things· had· gone on from bad to worse, until I felt that we had reached the end of our rope on the plan of operations we had been pursuing; that we had about played our last card, and must change our tactics, or lose the game. I now determined upon the adoption of the emancipation policy; and without consultation with or the knowledge of the Cabinet, I prepared the original draft of the proclamation, and, after much anxious thought, called a Cabinet meeting upon the subject. This was the last of July, or the first part of August, 1862. This Cabinet meeting took place upon a Saturday. All were present, excepting Mr. Blair, the postmaster-general, who was absent at the opening of the discussion, but came in subsequently. I said to the Cabinet that I had resolved upon this step, and had not called them together to ask their advice, but to lay the subject-matter of a proclamation before them; suggestions as to which would be in order after they had heard it read. Mr. Lovejoy was in error when he informed you [viz., Mr. Carpenter, at a previous time] that it excited no comment, excepting on the part of Secretary Seward. Various suggestions were offered. Secretary Chase wished the language stronger in reference to the arming of the blacks; Mr. Blair, after he ' came in, deprecated the policy on the ground that it would cost the Administration the fall elections.

---

* Six Months at the White House, pp. 20, 21, 22.

Nothing, however, was offered that I had not fully
anticipated and settled in my own mind, until Secretary
Seward spoke. He said in substance: 'Mr. President,
I approve of the proclamation, but I question the expediency of its issue at this juncture. The depression of
the public mind, consequent upon our repeated reverses,
is so great that I fear the effect of so important a step.
It may be viewed as the last measure of an exhausted
government; a cry for help; the government stretching forth its hands to Ethiopia, instead of Ethiopia
stretching forth her hands to the Government.' His
idea was, that it would be considered our last shriek on
the retreat. 'Now,' continued Mr. Seward, 'while I
approve the measure, I suggest, sir, that you postpone
its issue until you can give it to the country supported
by military success, instead of issuing it, as would be
the case now, upon the greatest disasters of the war.'
The wisdom of the view of the Secretary of State
struck me with very great force. It was an aspect of
the case that, in all my thought upon the subject, I
had entirely overlooked. The result was that I put
the proclamation aside, as you do your sketch for a
picture, waiting for a victory. From time to time I
added or changed a line, touching it up here and there,
anxiously watching the progress of events. Well, the
next news we had was of Pope's disaster at Bull Run.
Things looked darker than ever. Finally came the
week of the battle of Antietam. I determined to wait
no longer. The news came, I think, on Wednesday,
that the advantage was on our side. I was then stay-
ing at the Soldiers' Home. Here I finished writing the
second draft of the preliminary proclamation; came up

on Saturday; called the Cabinet together to hear it, and it was published the following Monday."

At the final meeting of September 20th, another interesting incident occurred in connection with Secretary Seward. The President had written the important part of the proclamation in these words:

"That, on the first day of January, in the year of our Lord one thousand eight hundred and sixty-three, all persons held as slaves within any State or designated part of a State, the people whereof shall then be in rebellion against the United States, shall be then, thenceforward, and forever FREE; and the Executive Government of the United States, including the military and naval authority thereof, will *recognize* the freedom of such persons, and will do no act or acts to repress such persons, or any of them, in any efforts they may make for their actual freedom." "When I finished reading this paragraph," resumed Mr. Lincoln, "Mr. Seward stopped me, and said, 'I think, Mr. President, that you should insert after the word *"recognize,"* in that sentence, the words *"and maintain."*' "I replied that I had already fully considered the import of that expression in this connection, but I had not introduced it, because it was not my way to promise what I was not entirely *sure* that I could perform, and I was not prepared to say that I thought we were exactly able to 'maintain' this."

"But," said he, "Seward insisted that we ought to take this ground; and the words finally went in!"

Mr. Lincoln, having finished this account, explained in detail how the Cabinet and he were grouped at that meeting; and when the artist showed the Presi-

dent a pencil sketch of the picture as he had already
planned it, it was found altogether in accordance with
the facts, except that the whole composition had to be
turned end for end, in order to put Mr. Lincoln at the
right place, by the table.

The remaining necessary details of sketching were
now promptly completed; the painter's easel was set
up in the library, but shortly removed to the state
dining-room, where the work was finished. The painter
was in good earnest "turned in loose," for he was,
during the succeeding six months, on terms almost as
intimate with Mr. Lincoln as were the President's own
private secretaries. He went and came at pleasure,
sat in Mr. Lincoln's private office while confidential
business was transacting, and when any one looked
suspiciously toward him, the President would say,
"Oh, you needn't mind him—he is a painter." From
time to time the President and the members of the
Cabinet gave sittings for their respective portraits,
chatting easily and freely with the companionable
artist on all manner of topics, and exchanging all sorts
of reminiscences, stories, reasonings, and opinions.
Frequently visitors at the White House came to observe the progress of the great picture; at other times
friends of the artist, sometimes brought in by Mr.
Lincoln.

The industry of the artist was unfailing and ardent.
His relaxation even was part of his work, for it consisted almost entirely of cultivating a more perfect
acquaintance with the men whom he was to paint. All
day he worked at his designing, sketching, or painting, and all day was not enough. When night fell, he

lighted up the great chandelier of the room, and often labored straight onward, unconscious of the passage of time, until the morning light found him still brush in hand before the immense canvas, and drove him away by spoiling the tone of the gas-light.

At the end of a half year the work was completed, and the President and Cabinet, at the close of a business session, adjourned to the temporary studio, to hold a formal critical session upon the great picture. Sitting in the midst of his chief assistants, Mr. Lincoln pronounced what he called his "unschooled" opinion of the work, in words which Mr. Carpenter has not put on record, but which, he says, "could not but have afforded the deepest gratification to any artist." For two days before being removed, the picture was now exhibited freely to the public, in the East Room, several thousands of persons crowding in to see it on each day. On the last afternoon, the President and the painter went together to have a last look at the work before it was rolled up for removal. Mr. Lincoln sat down before the picture and gazed silently at it. Mr. Carpenter remarked that he had worked out his idea, and asked for Mr. Lincoln's final suggestions and criticism. "There is little to find fault with," was the reply; "the portraiture is the main thing, and that seems to me absolutely perfect." They discussed the various accessories: the war maps, the portfolios, the map showing the distribution of slaves in the South, the book leaning against the leg of the chair, which was painted as if bound in "law calf." The title placed upon this was that of a work which Mr. Lincoln had used in preparing his proclamation—Whiting's "War

Powers of the President,"—and this not being a law book, the President requested that the coloring of the cover be changed accordingly. " Is there anything else that you would like changed or added ?" asked the painter. " No," was the reply, and the President continued, repeating the very expression which he had used on examining the first sketch, " It is as good as it can be made."

The painter took the opportunity to describe the enthusiastic feelings with which he had first thought of the picture, and in which he had labored upon it, and to thank Mr. Lincoln for his constant kindness in all their intercourse. Mr. Carpenter adds, " He listened pensively—almost passively, to me—his eyes fastened upon the picture. As I finished, he turned, and in his simple-hearted, earnest way said, ' Carpenter, I believe I am about as glad over the success of this work as you are.' And with these words in my ear, and a cordial ' good-bye' grasp of the hand, President and painter separated."

A single incident in the subsequent history of the picture may be mentioned here, which has the interest that always attaches to premonitions and signs, and illustrates Mr. Lincoln's personal popularity. Mr. Carpenter's picture was exhibited in the Rotunda of the Capitol during a few days just before Mr. Lincoln's second inauguration, and while it was being secured in its place, a number of persons were looking at it, among whom was a policeman of the Capitol squad. All at once a stray sunbeam glanced through the dome and settled full upon the face of the portrait of Mr. Lincoln, the rest of the picture remaining in shadow. It was a startling effect. The policeman pointed to it, exclaiming, "Look! that is as it should be. God bless him! may the sun shine on his head forever!"

Mr. Carpenter's great picture, of whose conception and execution the foregoing is a brief account, represents the Cabinet of Mr. Lincoln grouped around their chief as they stood or sat when he read the Proclamation to them. It shows their ordinary costume and their manner of carrying themselves; and the table, the chairs, the room and all its fittings and furniture of every kind, are represented without ornament or addition, exactly as they were at the time. The artist's friends frequently told him that his picture would look barren and commonplace unless he put in some urns, pillars, curtains, tassels, velvet table-cloths, American eagles, banners of our country, geniuses of liberty, or other unmeaning symbols not there; but he as often replied, with great good sense and correct feeling, that he would rather fail, while on the side of truth, by painting the scene as it actually was, than to succeed by doing what would be actual falsehood. He justly felt that he had no more right to vary from the facts in the case, than a rebel historian would have to assert that Mr. Lincoln assassinated J. Wilkes Booth. The interest of the scene, the truthfulness of its representation—these were the only means which he chose to use for producing an impression, and in thus choosing he was true to his own principles and to those of real Art. "Art," to use Mr. Carpenter's own words, "should aim to embody and express the spirit and best thought of its own age." To this end, when men and their actions are painted, the men should be delineated, clothed, placed,

and circumstanced as they actually were; not as the
painter may fancy it most impressive to imagine them.
Greenough's statue of Washington, in the Capitol
grounds, which Attorney-General Bates called "a very
good representation of Jupiter Tonans," is a terrible
instance of the opposite of Mr. Carpenter's idea. This
statue represents the Father of his Country seated in
the open air, and clothed in a sheet swathed round him
so as to leave him naked, or nearly so, from about the
waist upward—a costume in which General Washington never appeared in public. To put our first President into a garb which was an imaginary one eighteen
hundred years ago, is exactly such a blunder, only the
other end foremost, as that which a Dutch painter committed in painting Abraham on Mount Moriah, drawing a fine bead on Isaac with a horse-pistol, for the
purpose of sacrificing him. Mr. Carpenter had too
much sense and tact to fall into any such errors of time,
or errors of association either; and the very simplicity
and plainness of the furniture and fittings in his picture
constitute an important part of its value, because they
are an important part of its truth. A century from
this time it will be very interesting to know that thus
these men were dressed, and thus was their council
held, and their council-room furnished. But a fluted
pillar, a red curtain, an immense vase, could have in
such a place no meaning, purpose, or interest whatever, except to show the shallowness, ignorance, and
conventionality of the artist.

The arrangement of the persons in this picture was
such as to throw them into two groups, which may be
called radical and conservative, the former composed of

Messrs. Chase and Stanton; the latter of Messrs. Seward, Welles, Bates, Blair, and Smith. Mr. Lincoln sits between them, as if in the place of a point of union, but still nearest to the radicals. The positions of the individual men are further symbolical. Secretary Stanton, representing the military force of the Government, is at the President's right hand, in the foreground, and Secretary Chase, in behalf of the public purse, stands by his side. Secretary Welles, of the Navy, is at his left, and a little in the background, the navy being secondary to the army in importance in the struggle. And Secretary Seward, holding what is often called the premiership or prime-ministership, and by etiquette having precedence of the rest of the Cabinet, is accordingly placed in the center foreground. With hand partly spread and forefinger extended, Mr. Seward emphasizes his approval of the Proclamation to which he has just listened, but suggests that it "be postponed until it can be supported by military success." At the opposite or left-hand end of the table Attorney-General Bates, his arms folded, is thinking steadily upon the new questions of constitutional law which this Proclamation will call up; and Secretary Smith and Postmaster-General Blair stand together near him.

The "still-life" or accessory portion of the picture is also fully furnished with meaning. Over the mantle-piece is the portrait of Andrew Jackson, who, after smashing nullification, prophesied that the South would attack the Government again, and that the pretext would be slavery; as if he were here present in the spirit to witness the death-stroke of the enemy whose work he foretold in the flesh. Behind Mr. Chase is the picture of Secretary Stanton's predecessor in office, Simon Cameron, who was the first member of the Cabinet to avow the radical belief as to what should be done with the negro in the war. On the table before the President lies a parchment copy of the Constitution. Behind Mr. Seward is a portfolio marked "Commissions: War Department." Above this, on the table, is a map marked "Seat of War in Virginia," and another, leaning against the table, shows the density of the slave population in the various parts of the South. In the foreground is Judge Whiting's strongly argued book on the "War Powers of the President;" by its side, open on the floor, lies Story's "Commentaries on the Constitution," and in a corner is a newspaper, to remind the spectator of the newspaper press, and its great influence in the cause of emancipation.

Mr. Carpenter's work is truly a historical painting. It represents the significant point and moment of a historical event of the very highest importance. It does this by placing permanently on record the faces and forms of the men who did the work, as they gathered and consulted over the crisis. And this it accomplishes with the clearness, the largeness, the thoughtful truth and impressive moral power that belong to unaffected simplicity and strict and conscientious adherence to fact. Besides the technical professional value of the work as a specimen of composition, drawing, and color; besides its even higher value as a collection of faithful and successful portraits, it has and always will have the very much greater value of an impressive and expressive monument to the enfranchise-

ment of the negroes from slavery, and the greater en-
franchisement of the United States of America from
sustaining slavery.

It remains to bring the history of Mr. Carpenter's
great work down to the present time (December, 1866).
After being finished, the picture was exhibited to the
public in New York and Boston, and also in many of
the Western cities, with very great success. Previous
to the opening of the exhibition in New York, upon
the arrival of the picture from Washington, while re-
touching some injuries and remedying some defects in
minor details, Mr. Carpenter worked upon it for thirty-
six hours without intermission—a remarkable feat of
physical and mental endurance; and, it may be added,
a violation of natural laws for which he subsequently
suffered the penalty in a sickness which came near
proving fatal.

In Chicago and Milwaukie the picture was exhibited
for the benefit of the Sanitary Commission, fairs in
those two cities netting handsome sums in each place.
The re-nomination, re-election, and re-inauguration of
Mr. Lincoln for his second term aided from time to
time in maintaining popular interest in the picture.
While it was at Pittsburg the assassination of Mr. Lincoln took place, and public interest in this impressive
portrait of himself and his constitutional advisers, one
of whom, Mr. Seward, was also a victim to the conspiracy, rose to such a pitch that, once at least, the doors
of the exhibition room had actually to be closed, so un-
governable was the pressure. For about a year from
September, 1865, the picture was stored in Mr. Carpenter's studio. In the summer of 1866 the artist retouched

and cleaned it, and placed it on exhibition for a couple
of days in his native town, Homer, N. Y. The fellow-
townsmen of the painter, and the people of the vicinity
for miles around, crowded the exhibition room, and the
artist enjoyed the peculiar satisfaction of the prophet
who *does* attain honor in his own country.

It may interest the reader to know how so large a
canvas (it is fourteen feet six inches long by nine feet
in height) can be safely transported about the country.
This is accomplished by means of joints in the frame at
top and bottom, which allow the picture to fold over
upon itself from each end, thus reducing it within man-
ageable dimensions. Creasing is prevented by laying
a light and softly covered roller within the canvas at
each folding place, and the whole being firmly screwed
together and boxed, it travels in perfect security.

Soon after the completion of the picture, Mr. A. H.
Ritchie, of New York, the celebrated engraver, was
engaged to reproduce it upon steel, in the highest style
of the art. To facilitate this purpose Mr. Carpenter
painted a small copy of his large painting, of the exact
size of the proposed engraving—twenty-one by thirty-
three inches. The engraver had nearly completed his
work, after more than a year's constant labor, when the
building containing his office was consumed by fire.
The plate was saved through the wise precaution of
Mr. J. C. Derby, who was interested in its publication,
in having it stored nights in a fire-proof building; but
the small copy of the large painting, valued at $2,500,
was destroyed. This gave rise to a false report, widely
circulated, that the original painting was lost; this, unin-
jured, still remains in the possession of Mr. Carpenter.

Sympathizing, as Mr. Ritchie did, in the aim and object of Mr. Carpenter's great work, he carried into his engraving from it something of the same enthusiasm with which Mr. Carpenter was himself inspired. The result is an engraving which has been pronounced by high authority the finest work of its class ever produced in this country, and thus is placed within the reach of every loyal household in the land a treasure which must become more and more valuable with the lapse of time and the increasing glory of the republic.

4

IV.

LINCOLN.

ABRAHAM LINCOLN was born February 12, 1809, in what was then Hardin, now Larue, County, Kentucky, on Nolen Creek. His earliest ancestor who can be determined, moved from Berks County, Pa., to Rockingham County, Virginia, in 1750. Thirty years afterward, Abraham Lincoln, the President's grandfather, moved to Floyd's Creek, in Bullitt County, Ky., where he was killed by an Indian. His widow soon removed to Washington County. Her son Thomas married, in 1806, Nancy Hanks, a Virginian, and the couple moved to Hardin County, where Abraham was born. The boy was born to poverty and hard work. In 1816 he obtained a very little schooling, but it quickly ended, for the next year his father removed to Spencer County, Indiana, an unsettled region, where he built a log cabin. When Abraham was ten years of age his mother died. Although all his school-days together barely amounted to six months' time, still he worked at his studies until he could not only read, but could write letters, which made him quite a sage, and often a scribe (but never a Pharisee), among his neighbors. At nineteen, young Lincoln, with a companion, took a flatboat-load of produce to New Orleans and sold it. During the down trip the two navigators beat off seven negroes who attacked them with the design of capturing boat and cargo. In 1830 his father moved

again, to Macon County; next year the young man made
a second flatboat voyage to New Orleans, managing so
well that the owner who sent him employed him as
clerk and manager of a flour-mill. In 1832 young Lincoln enlisted as a volunteer in the Black Hawk war,
and was chosen captain of his company, serving faithfully, though he saw no actual fighting. Just after
the war he made his first entry into politics, by run-
ing for the State Legislature, as a Clay man in opposition to Jackson, and was beaten (the only time) in a contest before the people. In his own precinct, however,
he received 277 votes, out of the 284 cast. He now
opened a store, and got the postmastership of the village, but had to sell out; then tried surveying, but
became embarrassed again in 1837, and his instruments
were sold by the sheriff in execution. He had always
spent what time he could in reading and study; and
he now gave up the idea of business, and went to reading law, with a view to a legal and political career.
Beginning in 1834, he was elected to the State Legislature for four successive two-year terms, during which
he gained considerable reputation as a speaker and a
sensible man of business. In 1836 he was admitted
to the bar, and in 1837 he settled in Springfield. At
the end of his fourth legislative term, in 1842, he
declined a re-nomination, in order to bring up his law
studies; and in the same year he married Mary Todd,
daughter of Hon. Robert G. Todd, of Lexington, Ky. In
1844 he stumped Illinois and part of Indiana, for Henry
Clay, and in 1846 he was elected to Congress—the
only Whig from Illinois—and by the startling majority
of 1,511, where Henry Clay had only had 914 votes.

While in Congress, with constitutional discrimination about principles, he voted for all supplies needed to carry on the Mexican war, but always refused to vote that the war had been justly begun. He was a delegate to the convention which nominated Gen. Taylor, in 1848, and labored hard in canvassing for him. During this congressional term, Mr. Lincoln had frequently occasion to vote on questions involving slavery, and always voted for freedom. In January, 1849, he moved a bill to abolish slavery in the District of Columbia, but it was too soon for public opinion, and the bill failed. The Wilmot Proviso was often before the · House, in consequence of efforts to apply it to recently acquired territory, and as Mr. Lincoln afterward said, he voted for it, "in one way or another, about forty times."

At the end of this session, in March, 1849, Mr. Lincoln declined a re-nomination; and was during the year beaten as Whig candidate for United States Senator from Illinois. He now passed a number of years at home, practicing his profession, and enjoying an increasing reputation as a lawyer and politician. During this time he invented his "camels," or machine for carrying a ship over bars or obstructions, of which a model is to be seen at the Patent Office in Washington. This consisted of a couple of large cases that could be inflated somewhat after the fashion of a bellows. These were to be sunk empty, secured under the vessel, and then filled with air, so as to lift the ship.

The Nebraska Bill was passed May 22, 1854, and in the following autumn the Illinois Legislature was to choose a United States Senator in place of Gen. Shields, who had voted with Douglas for the repeal of the Missouri Compromise. It was important that Judge Douglas' own State should indorse his course, and he went himself into this canvass. So did Mr. Lincoln on the other part, and with the better fortune. He met Douglas in public debate, and it was generally conceded on both sides that he decidedly gained the advantage of him, powerful debater as he was. The result of the canvass was accordingly the election of an anti-Nebraska legislature, and the choice of that able man and unswerving friend of freedom, Hon. Lyman Trumbull, for United States Senator. Mr. Trumbull had been a Democrat; and Mr. Lincoln having been a Whig, the friends of the latter were disposed to contest this choice, and to insist that Mr. Lincoln should be Senator. But with self-denying wisdom, he used his own personal influence to carry the votes of his friends to Mr. Trumbull, and thus secured his election.

Mr. Lincoln's reputation was becoming national at the time of the Fremont and Buchanan campaign, and he had 110 votes for the nomination as Vice-President with Fremont, standing next to Mr. Dayton, who was the nominee.

By this time Mr. Lincoln and Mr. Douglas were the recognized leaders, in Illinois, on the two sides of the great political controversy of the day. As Mr. Raymond says, in his "Life of Lincoln," "Whenever Mr. Douglas made a speech, the people instinctively anticipated a reply from Mr. Lincoln." In June, 1857, Mr. Douglas made, at Springfield, that speech which publicly committed him to the support of the Lecompton Constitution and of the Dred Scott decision. Mr. Lincoln, two weeks afterward, replied in a speech at the same place, and these speeches were a sort of preface to the famous series of Lincoln-Douglas debates the next year, which firmly established Mr. Lincoln's reputation as a wise and just politician, and as a powerful speaker and skillful and ready debater. The two combatants were in that year candidates for the United States senatorship, to be determined by the Legislature then to be chosen. On one hand, Mr. Douglas' fortunes were staked on the election, because if his own State would not continue him in the Senate, he would evidently not be available on his intended further road as a Presidential candidate. And on the other hand, the Republicans of Illinois felt it supremely important to register the powerful voice of their great State in favor of freedom, and against the oppressive measures forced on the citizens of Kansas. Each of the candidates had already pretty well defined his position, as they had spoken thrice each in June and July of that year (1858); when, on July 24, Mr. Lincoln challenged Mr. Douglas to meet him in a series of public debates during the pending campaign. Mr. Douglas, after a correspondence which indicates some reluctance to venture on the contest, offered a programme of seven debates, in four of which he was to have the opening and closing turns, Mr. Lincoln to have them only in the other three. But Mr. Lincoln, confident in his own plain, keen, and weighty reasoning, and straightforward, clear, common sense, and in the overwhelming justice and rightfulness of his cause, readily accepted the proposition, and the meetings were held.

The seven places of meeting were in as many different portions of the State, and the series of debates caused a very deep and genuine excitement. Each party greeted and welcomed and "celebrated" its champion by the ordinary means of marching in long rows, waving flags, employing brass bands, shouting, and firing of cannon. But these common and cheap manifestations were underlaid and intensified into a real meaning, by the confidence of each party in its champion, by a keen enjoyment on the part of the audience of every good point on a principle, and every successful hit at the opponent, and still more by the profound conviction everywhere felt that the rights of man and the foundation principles of American civilization were really in dispute. The result of the canvass was, that on the popular vote, the Republican vote was 4,144 more than that of Douglas ; but so shrewdly had the State been districted in the Democratic interest, that that party had a working majority in the Legislature, and Mr. Douglas was elected Senator. If Mr. Lincoln had succeeded, doubtless he would not afterward have become President.

The Presidential election, of November, 1860, was approaching. As early as in February of that year Mr. Lincoln was invited by the New York Young Men's Republican Club to speak in that city on the political issues of the times. This he did, at Cooper Institute, Feb. 27th; delivering a speech full of wisdom, knowledge, and unanswerable political and statesmanlike reasoning. That speech especially, in connection also with those afterward delivered in New England, gave Mr. Lincoln as high a reputation at the East as he had at the West.

The consequence of these speeches was undoubtedly that Mr. Lincoln was at least the second choice of the Chicago Convention from the start. He was nominated for President at Chicago on Friday, May 18, 1860, was elected Nov. 6, 1860, was re-elected in Nov., 1864, and having led the country successfully through the most powerful and dangerous rebellion of the world's history, was assassinated by J. Wilkes Booth on the evening of Friday, April 14th, 1865, and died early the next morning.

It is unnecessary to attempt here any formal account of Mr. Lincoln's actions while President, or of that vast expression of national mourning which attended his funeral *cortege* from Washington. to Springfield. The facts of the war, the facts of that unprecedented funeral, are sufficiently known. The purpose of the present sketch will be better served by an arrangement of some reminiscences and anecdotes of the man, so treated as to form an illustration of the principal points in his character.

Mr. Lincoln, as President of the United States, bore a load of responsibility and of difficulty beyond all comparison greater than was ever imposed not only upon any other President, but upon any other citizen of the United States as such. His vexations and perplexities find no parallel in our national history, except in those of Washington, as commander-in-chief and dictator during the Revolution. The great picture which this little book is meant to illustrate, commemorates the act which was the central and crowning one of Mr. Lincoln's official life, and he occupies by right the central place in the picture, his face wearing a characteristic expression of patience, melancholy, kindness, and perhaps a faint touch of humor. In his hand he holds the draft of the Emancipation Proclamation, which he has just read to the assembled Cabinet; and thoughtful and intent, he is listening with surprised interest—for he had never thought of the point before—to the weighty suggestion of Secretary Seward to wait for a victory.

The chief significance of Mr. Lincoln as a historical personage depends on his being a wonderfully true representative of the American character—that is, of the character of the American of the Northwest; for that region at this day controls the United States. It is as a representative man that he will possess the most just fame, and accordingly it is interesting to observe how the leading traits in his character as an individual correspond to the leading traits in our national character.

HONESTY.

A Mr. Crawford lent Mr. Lincoln, when a boy, a copy of Weems' "Life of Washington," which he was eagerly reading in the intervals of his labor. He left it through one stormy night so near the chinky wall of the log cabin, that the rain drove in upon it, soaked the book, and quite ruined its looks. Abraham was entirely without money, but with a natural rectitude perhaps equal to that of the hero of the spoiled volume, he promptly carried it to Mr. Crawford, showed it, told how the harm happened, and offered to work out the damage. Crawford, with good judgment, gave the honest little fellow the book, in return for three days' work at pulling fodder; and the incident gained him the lasting esteem of the Crawfords and of the neighborhood.

An entirely similar mixture of rectitude and independence of character was shown in the account given by Pollard Simmons about a county survey. Simmons, it appears, met General Ewing (in charge of the United States Surveys in the Northwest Territory), while Mr. Lincoln was a needy young man, and asked for a job for him. The General looked into his papers, and said that such a county needed surveying; Mr. Lincoln might do that; the pay would be $600. Simmons, in great delight, told young Lincoln the great news as soon as he got home, and was astounded to hear him reply that he didn't think he would undertake the job. "In the name of wonder, why?" asked poor Simmons; "six hundred dollars doesn't grow on every bush out here in Illinois!" "I know that," was the answer, "and I need the money bad enough, Simmons, as you know; but I never have been under obligations to a Democratic administration, and I never intend to be as long as I can get my living another way. General Ewing must find another man to do his work."

When Mr. Lincoln was a practicing lawyer, a post-office agent came in one day and asked for him. On finding him, the agent said he wanted to collect a sum of money due the Department since the office at New Salem was discontinued. Mr. Lincoln—for he was the ex-postmaster of New Salem—looked a little puzzled, and a friend who was present, seeing this, offered to furnish the money, but Mr. Lincoln, suddenly rising, went and fished out a little old trunk from a pile of books, and asked the agent what was the amount of his demand. The man told it—it was over seventeen dollars. Mr. Lincoln unlocked the trunk, took out a parcel of coin done up in a rag, opened it, counted it, and handed it to the agent. It was the exact sum. "I never use any man's money except my own," said Mr. Lincoln, when the agent had left. Though he had passed through much poverty and privation since leaving the post-office, he had always had that money ready in the rag.

He found no difficulty in applying his principle to the famous lawyer's problem, of "How to do right when you know your client is in the wrong." On this point Mr. Lincoln seems never to have satisfied himself with the common arguments that "the client may be right after all; that every man has a right to have his side stated as well as it can be, and the other client will have his side stated so; that the best plan for the judge or jury is to have the two sides each stated at their best, each without reference to the other." These reasonings, which lead easily to sophistications, tricks, and lies, Mr. Lincoln never relished; and his less squeamish colleagues used to say that he was even "perversely honest." It was perfectly well known that if he found himself on the wrong side, his help was worth little. He could not put his heart into an unjust cause. He would never engage on the wrong side if he could find it out, but made it a rule to determine the right and wrong of the case before taking it up, and if the client was wrong, he refused the work and the fee, and told the applicant that he had no case, and ought not to go to law. Clients will sometimes fool their own lawyers and deceive them about the case.

Mr. Lincoln was once or twice so dealt with; but even in the middle of the suit, if the testimony revealed such a fact, the whole audience could see Mr. Lincoln's interest in his case fall and die, and the rest of his labor in it was merely formal. On one such occasion, where he had an associate counsel, Mr. Lincoln promptly informed him that he should not make the argument in the case; the associate made it, won the cause, received the fee—nine hundred dollars—and offered Mr. Lincoln his share. The upright lawyer would not touch a cent of it. He was once defending a person who had delivered certain lambs where sheep were contracted for. This fact did not appear until the testimony showed it on the trial. When that happened, Mr. Lincoln simply examined the witnesses to find how many such lambs were delivered, and when he addressed the jury, he plainly told them that their business was to give a verdict against his client, and that all he asked of them was to judge justly as to the extent of damages. In another case he had successfully sued a railroad company, and was about to have judgment, a certain offset being proved against his client, which offset was of course to be deducted from the amount of the judgment. But just in time to correct an error, the honest lawyer rose and informed the court that the offset against his client ought to be larger by such and such a sum, which he proceeded to describe and allow; and the court deducted it accordingly. It is no wonder that such a man was called "perversely honest." He was a capital lawyer for honest men, but a miserable lawyer for scoundrels.

A similar scrupulous honesty was shown in his habit

of dividing joint fees when he received them. He always did this with each separate fee, setting his associate's portion aside in its own parcel, with the owner's name and that of the case in which it was received. This was only a habit, but it strongly marks the principle.

This ingrained instinctive honesty was, however, a principal element of his power as a lawyer and as a speaker. What jury could resist a prepossession to begin with, in favor of a man who, it was perfectly notorious, always refused cases he did not believe in? No man alive could help being disposed to give him a verdict under such circumstances. What listener before the orator's platform could help feeling the influence of the visible effort to state the exact truth, which so singularly fills period after period of all Mr. Lincoln's arguments? The contrast between his painfully earnest, homely, direct struggle after mere fact as such, and the skillful contrivances of the trained politician's efforts to make out a case, is wonderfully clear in the speeches of the great series of debates with Mr. Douglas. As the reader passes from one to the other and back again, he feels a change of moral atmosphere, almost like that of alternating between a juggler's gaslit exhibition-room and a cool sunshiny morning landscape.

Before delivering that speech at Springfield which so clearly and ably defined the essence of the whole question of slavery and anti-slavery, Mr. Lincoln made an experiment on his law partner, Mr. Herndon, which showed the same honesty in arguing a political point as he used in arguing a legal point. Just before going to the meeting he locked himself in with Mr. Herndon, and reading him the first paragraph of the speech, asked, "What do you think of it?" "I think it is all true," was the reply, "but I doubt whether it is good policy to say it now." "That," said Mr. Lincoln, "makes no difference. It is the truth, and the nation is entitled to it."

The utter and uncompromising honesty of the man soaked and colored all his life. It was as quietly prompt and effective on the question of the Presidential nomination as on the question of the old rain-sopped book. They telegraphed to him when the Chicago Convention was in session, that to carry the Convention he must have the votes of two delegations named, and that for this he must pledge himself if elected to put the chiefs of those delegations into his Cabinet. He spoke instantly back by the wires, with Lincolnian morals and phrase, "I authorize no bargains, and will be bound by none."

COURAGE.

Mr. Lincoln possessed abundance of courage, both physical and moral; but of his physical courage it is to be remarked that it was much more likely to be aroused by offenses against honor or by abuses practiced on the defenseless than by any impositions on himself. He was far from being a fighter like General Jackson; and in fact so predominant was his kindliness and shrinking from causing pain to others, that he only bestirred himself when driven to the farthest endurable limit. On one of his flatboat trips to New Orleans he and his sole companion, armed with billets of wood,

met and thoroughly thrashed and defeated seven negroes, who made a night attack on their boat. When
he kept a little grocery, and a local bully used some
coarse language before some women, Lincoln asked
him to refrain, and being rudely challenged in consequence, wrestled with the fellow, threw him, and with
an odd, grim jocularity held him down and rubbed
smartweed into his face and eyes until he roared in
agony. But then releasing him, he at once did all in
his power to relieve the pain, with so much genuine
good-nature that the beaten bully became his life-long
friend. When a gang of roughs in the neighborhood
forced him into a contest with their champion, and closing on him in the struggle jointly leveled him to the
earth as he was winning in the combat, he was neither
enraged nor scared, but jumped up, joked over his own
defeat, and by sheer good-nature made them all so
much his friends that they invited him to become of
their worshipful company. This honor he thankfully
declined, but retained their friendship. Once when a
gang of political roughs threatened and attempted to
drive Colonel Baker off a platform, Mr. Lincoln unex-
pectedly dropped down through a scuttle in the ceiling
to Colonel Baker's side and coolly observed, " This is a
land of freedom of speech. Mr. Baker has a right to
speak. No man shall take him from the stand if I can
prevent it." And they gave up the attempt. When
Mr. Linder, a powerful speaker, had been threatened
with violence for things uttered in a speech that was
disagreeable to the Democrats, Mr. Lincoln and Colonel Baker alone escorted him safe home to his hotel,

Plots and plans for the assassination of Mr. Lincoln

were diligently contrived from the time of his first nomination at Chicago until the final successful attempt in
1865. So many letters did he receive which threatened his life, that he kept a separate file of them. "The
first one or two," he said to Mr. Carpenter, "made me
feel a little uncomfortable, but I came at length to look
for a regular installment of this kind of correspondence
in every week's mail, and up to inauguration-day I was
in constant receipt of such letters. It is no uncommon
thing to receive them now [March, 1864, the year before his death], but they have ceased to give me any
apprehension." When the artist expressed his surprise
at this, Mr. Lincoln answered, after his quaint fashion,
"Oh, there's nothing like getting used to things!"
When he left home for his first inauguration, an attempt
was made to throw the train from the track; then a
hand-grenade was found secreted in the cars; then an
organization to assassinate him was found to exist at
Baltimore. Yet he deviated not one inch from his proposed route, with the sole exception that he went from
Harrisburg to Washington one train earlier than had
been intended. He hoisted the flag at Philadelphia,
spoke at Harrisburg, and moved and acted in all other
particulars exactly on the pre-arranged plan, as if no-
body could be killed by violence. All the arguments
and remonstrances of his friends at Washington failed
to reconcile him to the presence of the escort that prudence did in fact require. When General Wadsworth
on one occasion sent such an escort, in part actually
against his will, he complained that Mr. Lincoln and he
"couldn't hear themselves talk" for the rattle of sabers
and spurs, and that he was much more afraid of being

shot in consequence of the inexperience of some green cavalryman than of being seized by any of Jeb Stuart's troopers. He used to walk and ride about Washington at all hours, by day or by night, alone or with some single friend; and Colonel Halpine, then on General Halleck's staff, over and over again reminded his superiors of the total defenselessness of the President. "Any assassin, or maniac," says Colonel Halpine, "seeking his life, could enter his presence without the interference of a single armed man to hold him back. The entrance doors, and all doors on the official side of the building, were open at all hours of the day, and very late into the evening; and I have many times entered the mansion and walked up to the rooms of the two private secretaries as late as nine or ten o'clock at night, without seeing or being challenged by a single soul." Mr. Lincoln was convinced that his death would not help the rebels, and he seemed to think that they would reason in like manner, and not seek his life. The ease with which such reasonings satisfied him shows that he was brave enough, but the mistake was sadly demonstrated by the fact that he was killed in just the way he thought out of the question, when there was no longer any rebel confederacy to encourage, and by exactly such means as a proper escort would have effectually prevented.

Mr. Lincoln's moral courage was even greater than his physical. Indeed, he said that he thought himself a great coward physically—though he was certainly partly at least in jest—and he added, "Moral cowardice is something which I think I never had."

While Mr. Lincoln was practicing law in Springfield,

the other lawyers in that city had, most of them, some
political ambition, and accordingly they were shy of
any legal business likely to make them unpopular,
and particularly of defending men accused of helping fugitive slaves to escape. At that time it was com-
monly considered in that region that catching and sur-
rendering "fugitives from labor" was a constitutional
duty to be performed with alacrity. Even that high-
spirited man Edward D. Baker—afterward killed at
Ball's Bluff—in those days, when applied to profession-
ally by a person sued for helping off a fugitive slave,
plainly refused, and said openly that he could not afford
it as a political man. The defendant then consulted an
anti-slavery friend, who at once recommended Lincoln.
" *He's* not afraid of an unpopular case," said he;
" when I go for a lawyer to defend an arrested fugitive slave, other lawyers will refuse me; but if Mr.
Lincoln is at home, he will always take my case."

Having made up his mind what was the real scope
and bearing of the political controversy which Mr.
Douglas was trying to conduct on his " popular sovereignty" principle exclusively, Mr. Lincoln had not only
the foresight to judge correctly what course was best
for the political future, and the rectitude to unreserv-
edly adopt that course as his own on principle, but the
moral courage—in his Springfield speech of July, 1858
—to avow the whole, clear, broad grounds of this line
of action, when even the party and personal friends
who were putting themselves into his hands by nominating him for the senatorship, judged that it would
be better to be silent. How just his perceptions were,
and how truly the heart of the people responded to the

key-note which he struck, was splendidly shown by his actually beating Mr. Douglas on the popular vote, though he failed of a majority and was "gerrymandered" out of an election in the Legislature.

When he became President, his moral courage was certainly not less required nor less conspicuous. Without experience in war, diplomacy, or high executive office, he found himself obliged to assume the responsibility of taking prompt and very critical and important steps in all three. Only waiting to discover what needed to be done, he did not fail to do it when the right time came. He called out seventy-five thousand volunteers; he blockaded the Southern ports; he seized all the telegraph dispatches on file in all the offices of the country for a year back; and did other acts of like kind, for which there was not, strictly speaking, any legal authority. It is true that these measures were necessary, were so jugded by the Cabinet, and were morally certain to be legalized by Congress; but would Mr. Buchanan have had the moral courage to do them? By no means; and the burden of their responsibility was a grave one even for the strong shoulders of Mr. Lincoln.

The same perfectly cool moral courage, acting always with a careful waiting upon the dictates of his slow and patient and fearless judgment, but acting with the most perfect promptness when the time came, was evident on many a subsequent occasion. Whether he acted or refrained from acting, neither the threats and abuse of enemies, nor the anger and impatience of friends, nor any fear of the face of man moved him. He wanted no help in doing right—he only wanted consultation to convince him what right was. When a foolish staff-officer, Major Key, had the insolence to tell him to his face that the generals in the field had a political policy of their own not to win battles, he instantly dismissed him from the service. When he thought best to prepare his Emancipation Proclamation he did so, and this time without asking advice of anybody. Just as steadily he postponed issuing it until the right day, and just as promptly, when that day came, he sent it forth.

WRATH.

Long-suffering and kindly as he was, Mr. Lincoln could become powerfully angry. This, however, was far harder where only he himself was concerned, than where his country, some important and highly valued interest, a friend, or some lowly and helpless person were concerned. A poor negro steamboat-hand, from Springfield or the vicinity, had been imprisoned in New Orleans, merely for being a free negro from out of the State, and was in danger of being sold for jail fees. Mr. Lincoln, finding that the Governor of Illinois had no power to do anything to prevent this rascality, jumped up, exclaiming, "By the Almighty, I'll have that negro back, or I'll have a twenty years' agitation in Illinois, until the Governor *can* do something in the premises." And he would have done it, had not some money been sent forward in time to rescue the poor fellow. The strongest expression of indignation that Mr. Carpenter ever heard him use was with reference to the Wall Street gold-gamblers, about the time of the Proclamation. "For my part," he exclaimed to Governor Curtin, and striking the table with his clinched fist, "I wish every one of them had his devilish head shot off!" An officer deservedly dismissed the service tormented the President with repeated statements of a case that was bad on his own showing, and on his third visit was impudent enough to say, " Well, Mr. President, I see you are fully determined not to do me justice!" Mr. Lincoln, his lips slightly closing together, quietly rose up, laid down the papers in his hand, seized the fellow by the coat-collar, walked him by main strength to the door and flung him into the passage, saying, "Sir, I give you fair warning never to show yourself in this room again—I can bear censure, but not insult!" Once at least, when some rebel women were impudent to him, he ordered them peremptorily to be shown out of the house.

DESPONDENCY.

The profound despondency which sometimes seized Mr. Lincoln was no disproof either of his strength and courage, or of his firm faith in the right. Such temporary affections were in part constitutional—for a vein of melancholy ran through his character—and were in part the result of the long and terrible draughts of the war upon his physical and mental forces. One day, in the midst of reports from the Wilderness battle-ground, Mr. Lincoln, with a face, tone, and manner of profound sadness and doubt, said to one of his personal and political friends, " Has it ever occurred to you that in view of the bad fortune that we have suffered so often and so long, and in such important instances, it may be that after all we are perhaps in the wrong? That the Lord is showing us that we are wrong?" And the friend answered him with similar sentiments, " Yes, it has, a

great many times." Yet such feelings never varied the
direct line of his public policy or of his public utterances.

INDUSTRY—PERSEVERANCE.

Mr. Lincoln was industrious and persevering. Indeed, like other self-made men, had he not possessed a
remarkable share of those qualities, he would have remained obscure. He was almost as poor as poor can
be. His father's whole estate, when they removed to
Indiana, was worth just about $300, and two thirds of
this was lost by a capsize in the river while moving.
The boy grew up in a sheer necessity of severe, un-
taught hard labor. In this his strength was consumed.
His whole "education" covered just over one year of
school attendance, and that at little district schools—and
scatteringly, here a little and there less, so as to make the
total as ineffective as possible. But with his own deliberate slow strength, he toiled with immense toil after
what he felt was lacking. Reading whatever good books
he could grasp, he wrote out a careful analysis of each
after finishing it—a task which few would ever begin,
and only the fewest of the few would ever continue or
complete. Pollard Simmons, a work-fellow with him
in his youth, thus reported of him on this point, in 1856
or thereabout: "Abe Lincoln was the likeliest boy in
God's world. He would work all day as hard as any
of us, and study by fire-light in the log-house half the
night, and in this way he made himself a thorough
practical surveyor."

He passed one summer and fall as "hired man" with
a Mr. Armstrong; and his earnest and diligent studies
during that time so pleased his employer as to produce

an offer to keep the youth through the winter, while he should continue at work at his books. The offer was accepted, though only on condition that the boarder should work enough to pay for his board.

He always remained deeply conscious of the serious misfortune of his early lack of culture; and with the same steady, deliberate, ceaseless effort sought to make up for it. He was "always thinking," the Illinois lawyers said; and he was reckoned an "improving man." From the time of his election to the Presidency he never knew what real rest or leisure was, but laboring up to the limit of his strength and far beyond it, he toiled straight forward, though conscious that he was exhausting himself. He had a distinct presentiment, which he avowed to more than one friend, that he would not outlive the rebellion, and he felt plainly that his labors were exhausting him. He had no fear of being murdered, and he undoubtedly felt that he was drying up the springs of his life by labor. He grew over-tired, wiry and powerful and enduring as he was. He remarked that such snatches of repose as he got "never reached the tired spot." During the last two years of his life, the progress of this exhaustion was shown by the perceptible coming on and increase of a certain nervous irritability, very far from his habitual quiet, easy kindliness of manner. But fresh or weary, his steady industry never once failed.

KINDNESS.

It seems scarcely possible for any human being to have been more thoroughly friendly, kindly, and free from hatred, revenge, jealousy, or ill-wishing than was

Mr. Lincoln. To many a woman and child, great and small, he was the same sweet-minded and beneficently · disposed man. Doubtless he wished as well to the rich and great as to the poor and helpless, but very naturally he found more good opportunities to help the latter, and more of them have been put on record.

The teacher of the Mission School at the Five Points House of Industry, in New York city, has given the following enthusiastic account of Mr. Lincoln's bearing even among children. It is a narrative of his visit to the school during his Eastern campaigning trip in 1860. "Our Sunday-school," says the teacher, "in the Five Points was assembled one Sabbath morning, when I noticed a tall, remarkable-looking man enter the room and take a seat among us. He listened with fixed attention to our exercises, and his countenance expressed such genuine interest that I approached him and suggested that he might be willing to say something to the children. He accepted the invitation with evident pleasure; and coming forward, began a simple address which at once fascinated every little hearer and hushed the room into silence. His language was. strikingly beautiful, and his tones musical with intensest feeling. The little faces around him would droop into sad conviction as he uttered sentences of warning, and would lighten into sunshine as he spoke cheerful words of promise. Once or twice he attempted to close his remarks; but the imperative shout of 'go on! oh, do go on!' would compel him to resume. As I looked upon the gaunt and sinewy frame of the stranger, and marked his powerful head and determined features, now· touched into softness by the impressions of the moment,

I felt an irrepressible curiosity to learn something more about him; and when he was quietly leaving the room I begged to know his name. He courteously replied, ' It is Abraham Lincoln, from Illinois.' "

Mr. Lincoln loved children and babies with a love much like that which women have for them. A woman whose husband was to be unjustly shot, had waited, her baby in her arms, for three days, in the President's ante-room, when Mr. Lincoln, in leaving his office for some refreshment, heard the child cry. He went straight back to the office, rang the bell for his usher, and said, "Daniel, is there a woman with a baby in the ante-room?" The usher said there was, and—knowing what was the poor woman's case—he added that her errand was one of life and death, and that he ought to see her. He ordered her instantly in; she told her story, and her husband was pardoned. As she came out of the room with her eyes lifted up, her lips moving in prayer, the tears streaming down her cheeks, old Daniel plucked her shawl and told her who was her advocate. "Madam," said he, "it was the baby that did it."

One of the editors of the Chicago *Tribune* says: " I dropped in upon Mr. Lincoln and found him busily engaged in counting greenbacks. 'This, sir,' said he, 'is something out of my usual line; but a President of the United States has a multiplicity of duties not specified in the Constitution or Acts of Congress. This is one of them. This money belongs to a poor negro, who is a porter in the Treasury Department, and at present very sick with small-pox. He is now in the hospital, and could not draw his pay because he could not sign

his name. I have been at considerable trouble to over-
come the difficulty and get it for him; and have at
length succeeded in "cutting the red tape," as you newspaper men say. I am dividing the money and putting
by a portion labeled in an envelope, according to his
wish.'" More than once he helped poor clients, not
only with free advice, but with gifts of money. During his great debates with Douglas, the two contest-
ants, with equally creditable good sense and good feeling, rode together to or from their appointments in the
same vehicle, chatting as pleasantly as if instead of
trying each to get into the Senate and keep the other
out, they were old friends meeting by pleasant chance.

The innate, irresistible, completely instinctive character of the kindness of Mr. Lincoln is, perhaps, most
strongly shown where it made him simply incapable of
acquiescing in or inflicting suffering at such; the impulse being as unreasoning as that which makes a
person jump away from a scald with boiling water.
Riding an Illinois circuit one day, he found a pig,
struggling in some deep mud, and evidently nearly exhausted; the sight hurt him, but having on a new suit
of clothes, he reluctantly rode on. But piggy had
got hold of the lawyer's heart-strings; the farther he
went the more uneasy he became, and at the end of two
miles he turned round, rode back, made a bridge of
rails out into the mud, dug out the pig, and then resumed his journey, with very muddy clothes, but with his
mind at ease. As characteristic as the kindness, was
the self-analysis that followed. He fell to considering
what his motive had been. At first he said to himself
that it was benevolence; but he concluded in the end

that it was selfishness; for he rescued the pig, he said, "in order to take a pain out of his own mind."

This irresistible shrinking from inflicting or allowing suffering, no matter for what purpose, was perhaps more strikingly exemplified in Mr. Lincoln's practice about the pardon of deserters and other convicted criminals, and on the military question of retaliation, than in any other case. The real justice of the case, the military bearings of it, the result of the decision on society, or the influence of his action on others tempted to imitate the offense, seemed to be considerations almost without weight in Mr. Lincoln's mind, in comparison with his invincible reluctance to inflict pain. The instinct was as unreasoning as would be that of a surgeon who should refuse to cut off a limb from dread of giving pain, even though the pain would save a life. Judge Bates said that he had sometimes told Mr. Lincoln that he was unfit to be trusted with the pardoning power, because he was so sure to be over-persuaded by beseechings, and particularly by the prayers and tears of women. Secretary Stanton and the generals in the field were often much vexed at having Mr. Lincoln mitigating or remitting punishments which they felt were indispensable for the good of the service. A well-executed representation of the sorrow of a deserter's or criminal's friends was all but certain to save the delinquent's life, and of course the result often was to turn a hardened scoundrel loose to prey on the community. When Mr. Colfax had specially urged the sparing of the life of a son of a certain constituent of the Speaker's, about to be shot for desertion, the President said, "Some of our generals complain

that I impair discipline and subordination in the army
by my pardons and respites, but it makes me rested,
after a hard day's work, if I can find some good excuse
for saving a man's life, and I go to bed happy as I think
how joyous the signing of my name will make him and
his family and friends." After pardoning, on his
mother's solicitation, a man condemned to death, the
President said: "Perhaps I have done wrong, but at
all events I have made that poor woman happy."

It is no wonder that doing such deeds transfigured
the gaunt and homely President into an angel of light
in the eyes of those whom he was blessing. On the
recommendation of Mr. Stevens, he had one day given
to an old lady a pardon for her son. In leaving the
White House, with Mr. Stevens, the old lady all at
once cried out, in an excited way, "I knew it was a
copperhead lie!" "What, madam?" asked her companion. "Why," she exclaimed again, with vehemence,
"they told me he was an ugly-looking man. He is the
handsomest man I ever saw in my life!"

Mr. Lincoln had some idea of his own weakness in
this particular. In a case of application to pardon a
man of previous good character, but sentenced for
manslaughter, the President replied, "Well, gentlemen,
leave your papers, and I will have the Attorney-General, Judge Bates, look them over, and we will see
what can be done. Being both of us *pigeon-hearted*
fellows, the chances are that if there is any ground
whatever for interference, the scoundrel will get off."

Even when the infliction of suffering was the only
and the sure way of saving far greater suffering, Mr.
Lincoln could not do it. One of his generals found

that deserters could not be shot, though desertion was actually seriously weakening the army; and he went to Washington and said so. "Mr. President," he urged, "unless these men are made an example of, the army itself is in danger. Mercy to the few is cruelty to the many." "Mr. General," said the President, "there are already too many weeping widows in the United States. For God's sake don't ask me to add to the number, for I won't do it." When ample and authenticated news was laid before him of the torturing of our men to death by slow starvation in the rebel prisons, Mr. Lincoln was profoundly moved. It was urged upon him, and justly too, that the only possible remedy was prompt and stern retaliation. But he said to Mr. Odell, "I can never, never starve men like that. Whatever others may say or do, I never can, and I never will be accessory to such treatment of human beings." Even further: after the awful devilism of the Fort Pillow massacre, and when in a speech at the Baltimore Fair he had pledged himself in public that there should be a retaliation for it, yet no step or move toward retaliation was ever taken. For Mr. Lincoln it was simply an impossibility. The extreme extent of this incapacity was assuredly a defect in Mr. Lincoln's character; but over-kindliness is not the fault which has done most evil in this world. Mr. Bates, in a conversation with Mr. Carpenter, once referred to this trait as the single flaw in Mr. Lincoln's character. "Mr. Lincoln," he said, "comes very near being a perfect man, according to my ideal of manhood. He lacks but one thing." "Is that official dignity as President?" inquired the painter. "No," was the reply, "that is of little consequence. His deficiency is in the element of *will.*" But this is not exactly the way to state it. The defect was based on two things: a too small faculty for feeling anger, and a too great and sensitive faculty for feeling the sufferings of others. He had will enough, but these two mental characteristics, standing behind the will, fixed it immovably in a resolution that he "never could and never would" do such and such things.

SIMPLICITY, UNAFFECTEDNESS.

A very prominent trait in Mr. Lincoln was his entire freedom from pride, affectation, assumption, or show of any kind. His ways were singularly unconscious, and even when any fact or characteristic of himself came in question, he recognized it or stated it exactly as it was, the mere fact appearing to be all that he required. He seemed not to remember, or at least not to care, how the statement of the fact was going to make him appear. One exception to this rule is on record; it was about his duel with General Shields. This duel was one of that numerous class of duels that did not happen; it only went so far as the sending of a challenge by the hot-blooded Irishman and its acceptance by Mr. Lincoln, who took the responsibility rather than allow the authorship of certain satirical verses to be charged to the real writer, a young lady, afterward Mrs. Lincoln. Mr. Lincoln chose broadswords as the weapons, because his arms were long, and he reckoned he could keep Shields off; but friends interposed on the ground, and a reconciliation was effected. Long afterward, at Washington, during the February before his death, a distin-

guished army officer, being at the White House, asked
Mr. Lincoln in conversation, "Is it true, Mr. President,
as I have heard, that you once went out to fight a duel
for the sake of the lady by your side?" The President's
face flushed, and he replied with a good deal of warmth,
"I do not deny it; but if you desire my friendship you
will never mention the circumstance again."

But Mr. Lincoln's total indifference—whether natural,
or acquired, or both—to the defects of his homely person, was a more characteristic illustration of his general
manner as to himself; he joked and told stories about
himself exactly as he did about anybody else. When
all ready for a state dinner, he held up his hands, all
"in pimlico" with white kids, and said with a laugh,
"There's one of my Illinois friends who never sees my
hands in that predicament without being reminded of
canvassed hams!" He used to tell the following story,
and to enjoy it, too: "In the days when I used to be
on the circuit, I was once accosted in the cars by a
stranger, who said, 'Excuse me, sir, but I have an
article in my possession which belongs to you.' 'How
is that?' I asked, considerably astonished. The stranger
took a jack-knife from his pocket. 'This knife,' he said,
'was placed in my hands some years ago, with the in-
junction that I was to keep it until I found a man
uglier than myself. I have carried it from that time
to this. Allow me now to say, sir, that I think you
are fairly entitled to the property.'"

It was with genuine fun and enjoyment that when
Mr. Carpenter was first introduced to him, Mr. Lincoln
teased him with the sudden question, "Do you think
you can make a handsome picture of *me*?"

When a foreign minister is presented to the President, a speech is usually prepared for the President to make, by the person in charge of foreign relations, *i. e.*, the Secretary of State. One day a green clerk was sent over with such a speech, and finding several public men with Mr. Lincoln, he came close up and said softly, as one does who wants to cover up the ignorance of another, " The Secretary has sent the speech you are to make to-day to the Swiss minister." But the President answered in a loud tone, to the horror of the poor clerk, "Oh, this is a speech Mr. Seward has written for me, is it ? I guess I will try it before these gentlemen, and see how it goes !" So he read it out with comical tones, and observed slyly at the end, " There ! I like that. It has the merit of originality !"

When Mr. Chase withdrew from the canvass of 1864, a good deal of public interest was excited by an editorial statement in the New York *Independent*, that Mr. Chase wrote the concluding paragraph of the Proclamation. A friend who thought that perhaps Mr. Chase had had the bad taste to set the story afloat, went to see the President about it. " Oh," Mr. Lincoln said, " Mr. Chase had nothing to do with it. I think I mentioned the circumstance to Mr. Tilton myself." He had taken the best sentence he knew of to end the Proclamation with, adding two or three words, and was simply well pleased to have it credited to its author. .

He never seemed to have any idea that his being President made it necessary for him to treat others differently, or to be treated differently by them, except so far as business or public interests made it necessary. When a poor man came to him in the grounds of the

White House with a trouble to be remedied, he borrowed card and pencil of by-standers, sat down on the stone coping of the next fence and wrote the order necessary to help the applicant. Some who stood by smiled at the informality of the attitude; his mind was simply bent on doing the right thing in the quickest way. This unceremoniousness of his was well exemplified in his reply to Lord Lyons, the bachelor English minister, at the state audience where the British nobleman announced the marriage of the Prince of Wales. Any one whatever of the other sixteen Presidents of the United States would have uttered a formal series of congratulations; it is not improbable that Mr. Lincoln had one, with what he once jocularly called "some of Seward's *poetry*" in it, neatly drafted by the Secretary, all ready in his coat-tail pocket at the time. But the President replied as friendly man to man, "Lord Lyons, go thou and do likewise!"

Mr. Raymond well states this curious want of any sense of official importance in Mr. Lincoln. He says, "It would be difficult, if not impossible, to find another man who would not, upon a sudden transfer from the obscurity of private life in a country town to the dignities and duties of the Presidency, feel it incumbent upon him to assume something of the manner and tone befitting that position. Mr. Lincoln never seemed to be aware that his place or his business were essentially different from those in which he had always been engaged. He brought to every question—the loftiest and most imposing—the same patient inquiry into details, the same eager longing to know and to do exactly what was just and right, and the same working-day, plodding, laborious devotion, which characterized his management of a client's case at his law office in Springfield."

FORESIGHT.

Remarkable care and thoughtful guardedness of language are striking features in Mr. Lincoln's state papers; their assertions and provisions were prepared with successful caution against any unnecessary collision with future events. Mr. Lincoln's greatest exhibition of this quality, however, was displayed in his early, clear, and positive understanding of the true scope and bearings of the political struggle which ended in the rebellion, both as a national matter and as restricted to Illinois. His speech at Springfield, in June, 1858, on accepting the nomination to the United States Senate in opposition to Mr. Douglas, was a remarkable instance of political foresight and intrepid plain speaking. This was the speech in which he avowed, "I believe this government can not endure permanently half slave and half free," and showed how Mr. Douglas and his party were steadily advancing toward legalizing slavery in all States of the Union. The bold avowals of this speech, like the great Proclamation which answered and decided its suggestions four years after, was deliberately prepared without consultation with any of his friends, and was only shown to his law partner, Mr. Herndon, just before the hour of delivery; and it a good deal startled and a little frightened many of the speaker's friends by stating then the views and doctrines which all patriots came swiftly up to, a couple of years later.

In a smaller matter, in this same campaign, Mr. Lincoln showed equal shrewdness and justness of insight. In the "seven debates" of that senatorial contest between Lincoln and Douglas, the latter had amused himself with a series of questions intended to plant Mr. Lincoln by means of his own answers upon an unpopular anti-slavery platform. By the answers, however, Mr. Lincoln told the truth and avowed his true position, without becoming unpopular; for the fact is, that in that controversy Mr. Douglas totally failed to discern the signs of the times; he did not see at all how the North was abolitionizing itself by a perfectly natural reaction against the aggressive measures of the South. After answering. Mr. Douglas' questions, Mr. Lincoln squared the account by proposing some in his turn, which were so framed that Judge Douglas was forced to answer them in such a manner as to show that his own "popular sovereignty" doctrine would upset the effect of the Dred Scott decision in the Territories. The question was this: "Can the people of a United States Territory, in any lawful way, against the wish of any citizen of the United States, exclude slavery from its limits prior to the formation of a State Constitution?" When Mr. Lincoln's friends found what he was going to ask, they begged him to refrain; "for," they said, "he will show that his doctrine of "squatter sovereignty" will nullify the Dred Scott decision, will thus satisfy public opinion on that point, and will be chosen senator." "That may be," said Mr. Lincoln; "but if he takes that shoot he never can be President." "But," they rejoined, "that is not your look-out. You are after the senatorship." "No, gentlemen," was the reply, " I am killing larger game. The battle of 1860 is worth a hundred of this." The point is perfectly clear now : if Douglas' answer should assert the power of the Dred Scott decision to establish slavery in territories, his Presidential vote in the North was gone; if he denied it, or even showed how to dodge it by means of " squatter sovereignty," the vote in the South was gone—or at least fatally weakened; and this last is exactly what happened. It is all clear now ; but it required very clear sight and very strong faith to see it so plainly and act upon it so decisively two years in advance.

MELANCHOLY.

Mr. Lincoln's strong enjoyment of fun and humor did not prevent his character from being distinctly marked with a deep vein of melancholy, a tendency to which is not unusual in persons of his physical characteristics. All his biographers agree upon this natural tendency; and the dreadful responsibility and exhausting labor of the war aggravated it. The risk of assassination does not seem to have troubled him at all, and yet a steady presentiment appears to have gradually settled upon him that he should not survive the war. " Whichever way it ends," he said to Mrs. Stowe, " I have the impression that I shall not last long after it is over." To another friend he said: " I feel a presentiment that I shall not outlast the rebellion. When it is over, my work will be done." Indeed, he is said to have expressed the same expectation to Mr. Lovejoy, and to other of his friends. But he was sad, even without this dim cloud of death hanging half visibly over him. One morning, after receiving some bad news,

Mr. Lincoln met Mr. Colfax, and told him, adding that he had neither slept nor breakfasted, and exclaimed, "How willingly would I exchange places to-day with the soldier who sleeps on the ground in the Army of the Potomac!" This occasional despondency was like the similar feelings that more than once overpowered General Washington, and the similarity even runs into expressions. Almost exactly the same thought was expressed by Washington in the dark days of the Revolution, when he said to a friend, "Such is my situation, that if I were to wish the bitterest curse to an enemy this side of the grave, I should put him in my stead with my feelings."

When on one occasion Mr. Lincoln was most strenuously begged by an energetic lady for a soldiers' hospital in her own State, at the North, she enforced her arguments by saying, "If you will grant my petition, you will be glad as long as you live." In answer, the lady says, "The President bowed his head, and with a look of sadness which it is impossible for language to describe, said, '*I shall never be glad any more.*'" In reply, she urged that of all men he would have most reason to be glad; but he answered, "I know, I know"—and he pressed his hand on his side—"but the springs of life are wearing away, and I shall not last."

Mr. Carpenter repeatedly speaks of the sadness of Mr. Lincoln's face. "In repose," he remarks, "it was the saddest face I ever knew. There were days when I could scarcely look into it without crying." And the same trait is shown by his literary preferences on the serious side. Shakspeare, whose wonderful union of sadness and mirth was so much like Mr. Lincoln's own,

was his favorite author; and Hamlet, the most thought-
fully melancholy of tragedies, had for him a peculiar
charm. The poem, " Oh, why should the spirit of mor-
tal be proud ?" so famous as a favorite composition of
his, and so widely believed to have been written by
him, is a contemplation of the shortness and vanity of
life. He once repeated to Mr. Carpenter these lines
from Holmes' "Last Leaf," as "inexpressibly touching:"

> " The mossy marbles rest
> On the lips that he has pressed
> In their bloom;
> And the names he loved to hear
> Have been carved for many a year
> On the tomb."

And he added, " For pure pathos, in my judgment,
there is nothing finer than those six lines in the English language." Here again it is observable that the
author, who suited him so well, is remarkable for that
same union of fun and sadness.

RELIGION.

Mr. Lincoln had not a natural tendency toward forms
or formality in religion any more than in composing a
state paper, answering an announcement of the marriage of a prince, or conducting a conversation. But
as he was naturally a most thorough realist or believer
in the substance and actual facts of things, so was he
a believer in the Christian religion, and a doer, to the
best of his ability, of the commands thereof. He considered himself a Christian, too. But a natural secre-
tiveness or disinclination to talk about what interested
him most profoundly, kept him almost always silent on

such topics; and this habit was probably strengthened by his living so much among rough people, and among sharp lawyers and busy politicians. He one day asked a pious woman to describe a true Christian experience. She answered, in substance, that it is a conviction of one's own sinfulness and weakness, and of one's personal need of the support of the Saviour; the feeling of the need of Divine help and consequent seeking the aid of the Holy Spirit for strength and guidance. The President's reply was a very distinct avowal of his Christian belief. He said: "If what you have told me is really a correct view of this great subject, I think I can say with sincerity that I hope I am a Christian. I lived until my boy Willie died without realizing fully these things. That blow overwhelmed me. It showed me my weakness as I had never felt it before; and if I can take what you have stated as a test, I think I can safely say that I know something of that change of which you speak; and I will further add, that it has been my intention for some time, at a suitable opportunity, to make a public religious confession." On another occasion, when some person had referred to the many silent and unknown prayers daily put up for him, he said, after referring to the strength which he had derived from believing that such prayers were made— and speaking with special deliberation and solemnity— "I should be the most presumptuous blockhead upon this footstool, if I for one day thought that I could discharge the duties which have come upon me since I came into this place, without the aid and enlightenment of One who is stronger and wiser than all others."

Mr. Lincoln's profound sense of the nearness and
efficient action of God was impressively shown in the
manner of his final resolution to proclaim Emancipation, as announced at the Cabinet meeting where it was
resolved on. He introduced the subject at that meeting by saying: " The time for the announcement of
the Emancipation policy can no longer be delayed.
Public sentiment, I think, will sustain it—many of my
warmest friends and supporters demand it ;" then in a
lower tone, as if speaking to himself, *"and I have
promised my God that I would do it."* Secretary
Chase, who was nearest to him, was the only one who
heard these last words at all, and he asked the President if he had correctly understood him. Mr. Lincoln
replied: " I made a solemn vow before God, that if General Lee was driven back from Pennsylvania, I would
crown the result by the declaration of freedom to the
slaves." The President's daily observance of family
devotions was just as sincere as his sanctioning a great
public act by a vow to God. The captain of his body-
guard, Captain Mix, a gentleman of culture and intelligence, said: " Many times have I listened to our most
eminent preachers, but never with the same feelings of
awe and reverence as when our Christian President,
his arm around his son, with his deep earnest tone, each
morning read a chapter from the Bible." The depth of
his belief in the Christian God appears from his circu-
lar of November 16, 1862, to the army, against Sab-
bath-breaking; in which he said, " The discipline and
character of the national forces should not suffer, *nor
the cause they defend be imperiled*, by the profanation
of the day, or of the name of the Most High."

MEMORY.

Mr. Lincoln had the same sort of memory for faces and names which is said to exist by hereditary descent and centuries of practice in the European royal families. While President, some one mentioned to him a Mr. C——; "I have known him now for almost thirty years," was the reply. "My first board bill in Springfield began *on the 15th of April*, 1837, and C—— came along about strawberry time." A gentleman on shaking hands with him one day, said, "I presume, Mr. President, that you have forgotten me?" "No," was the answer; "your name is Flood. I saw you last, twelve years ago, at ——," and he named the place and the occasion. His memory for miscellaneous and literary matter was almost as remarkable. When a clerk in Offutt's grocery, he is said to have been able to repeat the whole of Burns, and to have been hard at work in securing Shakspeare in the same repository. While President, he repeated on a casual occasion the soliloquy in Hamlet, and with remarkable justness of conception and force of expression. On another occasion he repeated in like manner the opening soliloquy of Richard the Third, and gave it an interpretation and significance quite different from the usual one, and very appropriate and striking. He even remembered, sometimes, the driest statistics. At receiving a deputation of bankers from several parts of the country, he observed to one of them: "Your district did not give me so strong a vote at the last election as in 1866." The banker thought the President was in error, and that the fact was the other way. "No," said Mr. Lincoln, "you fell off about six hundred votes;" and taking from a shelf,

the official canvasses of the two elections, he turned to
the name of the district and showed that it was as he
said. Only a very powerful memory, moreover, could
have retained and furnished that wonderful river of
stories which flowed through all Mr. Lincoln's talk-
ing.

ABSENCE OF MIND.

Mr. Lincoln was frequently so absorbed in solicitous
thought, intense mental effort, or, in the years of his
Presidency, painful revery or sorrowful reflection, as to
become quite unconscious of his surroundings. This
tendency was aided by his natural freedom from self-
consciousness. When he lived at New Salem he used
so often to pass his most intimate friends in the street
without noticing them, that people reckoned him crazy.
He often sat down at his own table without realizing
the place or the company, and ate mechanically. He
cared for eating, indeed, always, about as little as the
Duke of Wellington, and was far better pleased to
"browse 'round," as he called it one day at Washington,
than to sit out elaborate state dinners. Once, during one
of the official hand-shaking performances at Washington, an intimate acquaintance of the President shook
hands, spoke, and was saluted in the usual form, but
saw that he was not recognized at all, and so he stopped
short a moment and spoke again. This waked up the
President, who now recognized his friend, and seizing
his hand, shook it heartily, exclaiming, "How do you
do? How do you do? Excuse me for not noticing
you. I was thinking of a man down South." This
"man down South" was General Sherman, who, with

several other "men," was at that moment making a promenade from Atlanta to the sea.

HUMOR.

Decidedly the most prominent characteristic of Mr. Lincoln's mind was his extreme love for jokes, wit, humor, and fun, especially for "stories," and he is famous for the immense supply of the latter with which he used on all occasions to illuminate his arguments, point his satire, ornament the thread of conversation, or occupy any corner or hint on which a similitude or an illustration could hang. In giving a general view of his character, a few of his stories and sayings, and of anecdotes that illustrate his love of mirthful matter, must be given. To repeat all of them would fill a large book, and has in fact already filled much larger books than the whole of this one.

As early as in the Black Hawk war, in 1832, Mr. Lincoln's popularity with the soldiers of his company and with the other troops of the command was attributed to his "great physical strength, his excellent care of the men in his command, his never-failing good-nature, and his ability to tell more stories and better ones than any man in the service. This strong natural talent was most powerfully developed during Mr. Lincoln's long and active experience among the lawyers and politicians of Illinois; and his Presidential career afforded a thick-coming series of occasions admitting of illustration by all possible sorts of parables, sayings, and comparisons, of which occasions Mr. Lincoln took full advantage. We all remember how frequently this trait was made the mark for all manner of attacks, grave, satirical, and scurrilous. But so far from originating in light-mindedness, frivolity, or badness of heart, the fact is that the overburdened and heart-worn President used the momentary relief that such things gave him as a medicine, a rest, as he might have used sleep, could he have always commanded it. Sleep often refused to come; but there is no account of Mr. Lincoln's having failed to have a story whenever he wanted it. His old friend Mr. Arnold understood this, and said one day, on hearing Mr. Lincoln's hearty laugh: "That laugh has been the President's life-preserver." Mr. Ashley, an Ohio Congressman, did not understand the case so well one morning, when he called on Mr. Lincoln just after one of the disasters of the summer of 1862. The President began to tell some funny story, when Mr. Ashley, provoked, rose up, saying, "Mr. President, I did not come here this morning to hear stories. It is too serious a time." Without irritation, Mr. Lincoln at once answered, with entire seriousness: "Ashley, sit down. I respect you as an earnest, sincere man. You can not be more anxious than I have been constantly since the beginning of the war; and I say to you now, that were it not for this occasional vent, *I should die.*"

He always kept in his desk the latest humorous book of the day, and from time to time, when fatigued or troubled beyond endurance, he would take out his book and read a chapter or two, with as much relief—and of a great deal better kind—as a weary toper could find in his glass of bitters. One evening, when he was utterly worn out with office-seekers over and above his usual heavy business, a delegation of public men came in, having matters in charge which required much attention and the examination of many extensive documents. So, as if to stimulate him for a special effort, the President took a dram—of fun. "Have you seen the Nasby Papers?" he asked one of the party, at the same time shoving all the documents to one side. "No," was the reply; "who is Nasby?" Mr. Lincoln said he was a "chap out in Ohio," writing in the papers with the signature of Petroleum V. Nasby; and, he added, "I am going to write to Petroleum to come down here, and I intend to tell him that if he will communicate his talent to me, I will swap places with him." So he took out the pamphlet collection of the Nasby Papers, and read a chapter. All enjoyed it; and Mr. Lincoln, refreshed by his own enjoyment of it, and by theirs, too, put away the book, and instantly coming back to business and seriousness, took up the matter in hand with prompt earnestness.

Dr. Holland says that when the President called the Cabinet together to hear his Emancipation Proclamation, he began first of all by reading a whole chapter from "Artemus Ward, his Book," laughing so wholly and heartily at Artemus' nonsense that some of those present were much pained. If they were so, it was merely from not understanding Mr. Lincoln; for assuredly he was as earnest as any of them in the matter of the Great Proclamation itself. Still, few men could possibly understand that singular intimate mingling of humor and seriousness without injury by either to the other, which was a feature of Mr. Lincoln's mind, unless they possessed in some measure the same combination of traits. But this intermingling was very com-

plete; it was promoted by Mr. Lincoln's want of what
phrenology calls "self-esteem," and by his rough Western life among men who are no respecters of persons;
and it sometimes occasioned rather startling and heter-
ogeneous assortments of ideas in Mr. Lincoln's talk as
to both men and things. When Mr. Cameron left the
Cabinet, certain earnest persons wanted others to leave
too, and urged Mr. Lincoln to have it so. In reply he
told them how Joe Wilson found that skunks were de-
stroying his chickens, and, getting excited, went out one
night and shot *one*, but it was "eleven weeks before
he got over killing that one," and accordingly gave up
the hunt for the rest. But Mr. Lincoln and Mr. Cameron were very good friends, and he did not at all
mean that he thought Mr. Cameron a skunk who ought
to be shot, or the rest of the Cabinet skunks that it
was unsafe to hunt. Exactly like this in style was the
story with which he answered some gentlemen who
asked what he would do with Jeff. Davis? He told
them of a boy who bought a "coon" and led him about
with a rope, until the tormenting creature had scratched
half his clothes off and tired him completely out. When
a man found him sitting down, miserable and unhappy,
and asked him, "Why don't you get rid of your coon?"
the boy answered, "Hush! don't you see he's gnawing
his rope off? I'm going to let him do it, and then I'll
go home and tell the folks he got away from me!"
When Messrs. Wade and Davis published their violent
manifesto against him, he said it was not worth fretting
about, and told the story of the old man whose son
warned him not to eat the cheese, for it was full of
wrigglers. "Let 'em wriggle, my son," said the old

gentleman, chewing away, "I kin stand it if they kin!"
When he was urged in the beginning of the war to
send a great fleet down South to draw off the rebels
from before Washington, he said it was like the man's
prescription to relieve the girl at New Salem who had
a singing in her head. This was to put a plaster of
psalm tunes on her feet and draw the singing down.
When he was told that "firing had been heard in the
direction of Knoxville," he said he was glad of it, and
when some one intimated that it was rather singular to
be glad of what intimated that Burnside was in danger,
he said that he was like Mistress Sallie Ward, an old
neighbor of his, with a good many children. When
one of her young folks was heard crying, off in some
out-of-the-way place, she would remark, "There's one
of my children that isn't dead yet!" The parable of
the man who declined to swap horses while swimming
a river, which he used to illustrate the risks of taking
another candidate than himself in 1864, is known to
everybody. Of the same sort was his answer to the
inquiry which an earnest clerical friend made in the first
days of his administration, what his policy was going to
be on slavery. "Once," said he, "a young Methodist
preacher was worrying in the presence of old Father
B., lest a freshet in Fox River should prevent him from
filling some of his appointments. Father B. checked
him with his gravest manner. 'Young man,' said the
old minister, 'I have always made it a rule in my life
not to cross Fox River until I got to it.' And I am
not going to worry myself about the slavery question
until I get to it."

The same perfect fusion of joke and earnest, metaphoric illustration and weighty truth, was shown in innumerable repartees, remarks, and comments on all sorts of occasions, about himself, the war, politics, anything that came up. A famous definition of eloquence is, "Logic, red hot." Mr. Lincoln's idea of convincing was, "Truth, made funny." It was almost always by similitudes, in one form or another, that he enforced his meaning, or else by quaint and expressive metaphors from rustic life; more rarely in the form of wit. An instance of the latter is his reply to the clergyman who "hoped the Lord was on our side." "I am not concerned about that," was Mr. Lincoln's answer, "for I know that the Lord is always on the side of the right. But it is my constant anxiety and prayer that I and this nation should be on the Lord's side." This was a good specimen of grave and lofty wit, where a most weighty truth is conveyed in a keen and sharply put antithesis. There was, again, a somewhat unusually satirical edge in his short answer to an anti-slavery delegation which once urged upon him the instant adoption of the emancipation policy, and whose chairman, the well-known racy preacher, Rev. Dr. George B. Cheever, spiced his arguments, after his manner, with many Old Testament quotations. Mr. Lincoln heard it all through, meditated a moment, drew a long breath, and observed, "Well, gentlemen, it is not often that one is favored with a delegation *direct* from the Almighty!"

When somebody pressed him for a pass to go through the Union lines to Richmond, he said "it was useless; that he had already given passes to four hundred thousand men to go there, and not one had got there unless he was carried." A civilian, so ignorant of military affairs as not even to know what appointment he wanted, sent in a written request to be made "general." The President indorsed the paper, by way of explanation and joke together, "*Major*-general, I reckon. A. Lincoln." He called the Presidency of the United States "a scrape;" for when somebody sent him a fine new hat just after he was elected, he tried it on, and then turning to Mrs. Lincoln said, with a quizzical manner, "Well, wife, there is one thing likely to come out of this scrape, anyhow: we are going to have some new clothes!" There was a decidedly comic element in his sending Vallandigham over among the rebels; it made the Ohio "sympathizer" look ridiculous before the whole United States, and killed him completely, in a political sense; the punishment was so funny that it could not be whined over as a persecution. Of the same kind was the reasoning indorsed on the decision in the case of Franklin W. Smith; a document which the Navy Department *will not allow to be copied.* But it was very nearly thus: Smith, it must be premised, had been most vindictively pursued by a "military court," whose whole finding Mr. Lincoln annulled in the following quaintly reasoned indorsement:

" *Whereas*, Franklin W. Smith had transactions with the Navy Department to the amount of one million and a quarter of a million of dollars; and *whereas*, he had a chance to steal a quarter of a million, and was only charged with stealing twenty-two hundred dollars, and the question now is about his stealing a hundred—therefore I don't believe he stole anything at all. Therefore the record and findings are disapproved, declared null and void, and the defendants are fully discharged."

Having completed his second inaugural—which the

7

London *Spectator* called "the noblest political document known to history"—he brought it, on the Sunday
evening before the re-inauguration, into his office, where
several personal friends were sitting, and thus proclaimed its existence, and as much as he chose of its character: "Lots of wisdom, I suspect, in that document.
It is what will be called my second inaugural, containing about six hundred words." He always had a joke
for any actual or real misadventure to himself. When
beaten for United States senator, in Illinois, he was
asked how he felt about it, and replied that he "felt
like the boy who had stubbed his toe—too bad to laugh
and too big to cry." When some one brought him bad
news as to the prospect for his re-election, he said,
"Well, I can not run the political machine—I have
enough on my hands without *that*. It is the people's
business—the election is in their hands. If they turn
their backs to the fire and get scorched in the rear,
they'll find they've got to *sit on the blister!*" A judge
who had in vain asked General Halleck, and then Secretary Stanton, for a pass to go to Richmond, applied
to the President. "Have you asked Halleck?" said
Mr. Lincoln, "Yes, and met with a flat refusal." "Then
you must see Stanton." "I have," said the Judge,
"and with the same result." "Well, then," said Mr.
Lincoln, smiling, "I can do nothing; for you must
know, *I have very little influence with this administration!*" He remarked with a very quiet but very satirical quaintness one day, that if McClellan did not want
the army for anything, he "would like to borrow it."
He called his going to his work in the morning "opening shop." Speaking to Mr. Raymond in the begin-

ning of his term of the absurd situation he found himself in, with the rebellion upon him, and the horrible mob of office-holders that besets every new President howling and whining about him, and occupying so much of his time, he said, "I am like a man so busy letting rooms in one end of his house, that he can't stop to put out the fire at the other end." Having signed a great pile of commissions, he said to Mr. Carpenter, "There, I've got that job *husked out.*" These instances—a few only out of a whole life-full—are however enough to show how completely Mr. Lincoln's ways of thought and speech were homely, direct, metaphorical, and humorous or witty.

LANGUAGE—REASONING—ORATORY.

Mr. Lincoln was not a great orator, but he was a very convincing public reasoner, and his language, whether written or spoken—for they were exactly alike—as well as his modes of reasoning, had some noticeable peculiarities. Of these, the chief is, the clearness and force with which the thought is conveyed, notwithstanding what may seem awkward or undignified forms of expression. There is a curious contrast, which will strongly illustrate this point, between two passages conveying precisely the same idea; with one of which Daniel Webster opened his magnificent reply to Hayne, and the other is the beginning of Mr. Lincoln's great speech at Springfield, on opening the senatorial campaign against Douglas. The great Massachusetts orator began thus:

" When the mariner has been tossed for many days, in thick weather, and on an unknown sea, he naturally avails himself of the first pause in the storm, the earliest glance of the sun, to take his latitude, and ascertain how far the elements have driven him from his true course. Let us imitate that prudence, and before we float farther, refer to the point from which we departed, that we may at least be able to conjecture where we now are."

In his speech at Springfield, a singularly clear, terse, profound, and comprehensive statement of the slavery and anti-slavery controversy, Mr. Lincoln covers exactly the same ground, as follows :

" If we could first know where we are, and whither we are tending, we could better judge what to do, and how to do it."

Mr. Webster here used eighty-two words, of which twenty, almost a quarter, have more than one syllable. Mr. Lincoln used twenty-five words, of which three, or less than one eighth, have more than one syllable. This may seem a petty method of comparing orators ; but it reveals a great secret of directness, clearness, simplicity, and force in style—it goes far to explain how Mr. Lincoln convinced an audience. Of the same condensed sort was a little " sermon"—a very comprehensive code for living a good life, which Mr. Lincoln is said to have often repeated to his boys. It would be a good discourse for every boy in the United States to commit to memory—and still better to live up to. Thus it ran :

" Don't drink, don't smoke, don't chew, don't swear, don't gamble, don't lie, don't cheat. Love your fellow-men and love God. Love truth, love virtue, and be happy."

Almost as short was his first public political speech, in 1832, at offering himself for the Illinois Legislature.

His opponent had set forth his views at great length, and Mr. Lincoln, when his turn came, spoke thus:

"Gentlemen, fellow-citizens: I presume you know who I am— I am humble Abraham Lincoln. I have been solicited by many friends to become a candidate for the Legislature. My politics can be briefly stated. I am in favor of a national bank. I am in favor of the internal improvement system, and a high protective tariff. These are my sentiments and political principles. If elected, I shall be thankful. If not, it will be all the same."

As a reasoner to juries, Mr. Lincoln was very successful. One great cause of this, as has been shown, was the well-known fact that what he argued heartily he believed in heartily. Thus his client had, besides the justice of his cause, the whole weight of the lawyer's personal character—an advantage of vast importance, but which few lawyers know or care about. But all this was materially helped by the strenuous directness with which Mr. Lincoln labored straight at the truth— the facts—and the utter sincerity with which, when he had grasped them himself, he strove to communicate them to the jury in the plainest, simplest, clearest way. To be sure, he told stories and used humorous turns of expression. But these were so used as to be clear lights flung direct upon the point in hand—not, as with rhetoricians, mere fireworks to dazzle and confuse. After Mr. Lincoln's death, memorial proceedings of the usual kind were had in the courts of Illinois. Ex-Judge Caton, in the Supreme Court at Ottawa, in speaking to the resolutions from the bar, observed, "Mr. Lincoln knew the relations of things, and hence his deductions were rarely wrong from any given state of facts. So he applied the principles of law to the transactions of

men with great clearness and precision. He was a
close reasoner. He reasoned by analogy, and enforced
his views by apt illustrations." Judge Breese, on the
same occasion, said, "I have for a quarter of a century
regarded Mr. Lincoln as the finest lawyer I ever knew."
Judge Drummond, of Chicago, said, "He was one of the
ablest lawyers I have ever known." Long before he
became known in politics, he was pointed out to a
stranger by a citizen of Springfield as "Abe Lincoln,
the first lawyer of Illinois."

His success before popular audiences was based on
the same qualities as his success with juries. Both de-
pended upon his complete mental sympathy with average men, and his great power of stating and illustrating facts upon the mental level of average men—that
is, plainly, directly, forcibly, and humorously. An
account, by the Rev. J. B. Gulliver, of a conversation
with Mr. Lincoln, about his speech at Norwich, Conn.,
during his visit at the East just after the Seven
Debates with Douglas, gives so just and striking a
portraiture of Mr. Lincoln's speaking and modes of
thought, that it is transcribed here. It is from the
New York *Independent* of Sept. 1, 1864. Mr. Gulliver,
meeting Mr. Lincoln in the cars the day after the
speech, said, during the conversation, that it was "one
of the most extraordinary speeches he ever heard."

"As we entered the cars [continues Mr. Gulliver], he beck-
oned me to take a seat with him, and said, in a most agree-
ably frank way, 'Were you sincere in what you said about
my speech just now?' 'I meant every word of it, Mr. Lincoln. Why, an old dyed-in-the-wool Democrat, who sat near
me, applauded you repeatedly; and, when rallied upon his
conversion to sound principles, answered, "I don't believe a

word he says, but I can't help clapping him, he is so *pat!*"
That I call the triumph of oratory—

> "When you convince a man against his will,
> Though he is of the same opinion still."

Indeed, sir, I learned more of the art of public speaking last
evening than I could from a whole course of lectures on Rhetoric.'

" 'Ah! that reminds me,' said he, 'of a most extraordinary
circumstance which occurred in New Haven the other day.
They told me that the Professor of Rhetoric in Yale College—
a very learned man, isn't he?'

" 'Yes, sir, and a fine critic, too.'

" 'Well, I suppose so; he ought to be, at any rate—they told
me that he came to hear me, and took notes of my speech, and
gave a lecture on it to his class the next day; and, not satisfied
with that, he followed me up to Meriden the next evening, and
heard me again for the same purpose. Now, if this is so, it is
to my mind very extraordinary. I have been sufficiently astonished at my success in the West. It has been most unexpected.
But I had no thought of any marked success at the East, and
least of all that I should draw out such commendations from
literary and learned men. Now,' he continued, 'I should like
very much to know what it was in my speech you thought so
remarkable, and what you suppose interested my friend the
Professor so much.'

" 'The clearness of your statements, Mr. Lincoln; the unanswerable style of your reasoning, and especially your illustrations, which were romance and pathos, and fun and logic
all welded together. That story about the snakes, for example,
which set the hands and feet of your Democratic hearers in
such vigorous motion, was at once queer and comical, and
tragic and argumentative. It broke through all the barriers
of a man's previous opinions and prejudices at a crash, and
blew up the very citadel of his false theories before he could
know what had hurt him.'

" 'Can you remember any other illustrations,' said he, 'of
this peculiarity of my style?' .

"I gave him others of the same sort, occupying some half hour in the critique, when he said: 'I am much obliged to you for this. I have been wishing for a long time to find some one who would make this analysis for me. It throws light on a subject which has been dark to me. I can understand very readily how such a power as you have ascribed to me will account for the effect which seems to be produced by my speeches. I hope you have not been too flattering in your estimate. . Certainly, I have had a most wonderful success, for a man of my limited education.' "

Perhaps the most characteristic of all Mr. Lincoln's peculiarities of reasoning was his habit of arguing *against himself*—against the view to which he was inclined, which he desired, which he expected to adopt, and which he did in fact finally adopt. His widely-known saying, when urged by a deputation of clergymen to proclaim emancipation, "I do not want to issue a document that the whole world will see must necessarily be inoperative, like the Pope's bull against the comet!" was uttered more than a month after he had declared to the Cabinet his confirmed purpose to issue the Great Proclamation. While a lawyer, he used, in the words of Dr. Holland, to "study both sides (of his cases) with equal thoroughness. It was in the days of his legal practice his habit to argue against himself, and it always remained the habit of his life. He took special interest in the investigation of every point that could be made against him and his positions." Mr. Colfax, in his Chicago funeral oration upon Mr. Lincoln, thus described this trait:

"When his judgment, which acted slowly, but which was almost as immovable as the eternal hills when settled, was grasping some subject of importance, the arguments against his own desires seemed uppermost in his mind, and in conversing upon it, he would use those arguments, to see if they could be rebutted."

After the same fashion, although he was thought to hesitate a good while before he nominated to the place of Chief-Justice of the United States, vacant by Judge Taney's death, yet he said himself that "there never was a time during his Presidency when, in the event of the death of Judge Taney, he had not fully intended and expected to nominate Salmon P. Chase for Chief-Justice."

ORIGINALITY.

Mr. Lincoln's methods of thinking and ways of expressing his thoughts were so completely his own that his mental operations gave an impression of lonesomeness. The expedients he used, the thoughts that came into his mind, the phraseology in which he communicated them, were not only his own, but they were so different from what others would have thought of, that they surprise. This quality, indeed, had much to do with the impressiveness of his reasonings; an idea stated in a way that we never thought of before, is very hard to forget or to disprove. A curious illustration of this ready and out-of-the-way but sufficient suggestiveness is the story of his getting his boat over a dam. The boat was water-logged, and he got the bow over the dam, and then bored a hole through the bottom and let the water out, to lighten her. Other men would have bailed her out. Nearly all the anecdotes that have already been given to bring out other points in Mr. Lincoln's character, do in fact show also this same trait of originality. The punishment of Vallandigham—the " opening shop"—almost every act and word of the man, in fact, was of the same original, peculiar, and yet sufficient character. Nothing more strongly illustrates and proves this trait of originality than the fact that Mr. Lincoln said things that became proverbial. "If slavery is not wrong, nothing is wrong," he wrote in a letter; an expression which says, characteristically, in Mr. Lincoln's reasoning manner, what Wesley put more epigrammatically, but not more powerfully, when he said, "Slavery is the sum of all villainies." His great speech at New York ended with the lofty thought: "It has been said of the world's history hitherto, that ' might makes right ;' it is for us and for our times to reverse the maxim, and to show that right makes might." His phrase " to swap horses while crossing the river," is even more widely current, and the very noble antithesis in the second inaugural— " With malice toward none, with charity for all," is not only proverbial but historical.

EDUCATION.

Mr. Lincoln, as has been mentioned, had but few months schooling in all. He never read a novel; He read newspapers, and indeed may be said to have studied them, for a great part of his life, although after he became President he hardly looked into any. He found that facts themselves were all he could attend to, without trying to see what editors thought of them. He began " Ivanhoe" once, but did not finish it. The class-books he studied most were neither grammar nor geography, but the Bible, Shakspeare, Æsop's Fables, and the Pilgrim's Progress. Of the former three he could repeat considerable portions. And he read, also, the Life of Washington, the Life of Franklin, and the Life of Henry Clay. It would be very hard to choose seven better books for a young man to feed on. But Mr. Lincoln's real education was his life of strenuous mental labor, first in learning the principles applicable to his work, whatever that was, and secondly, in applying those principles so as to do that work in the quickest and most effective way.

PRESIDENT.

The merit of Mr. Lincoln's Presidency is, that he judged so well what the people of the United States willed, and when and how to do what they willed. If he had able advisers, so much the greater his merit for knowing good advice when it was given to him and for following it. It is exactly the proper office of an American statesman and ruler as distinguished from a monarchical one, that he must see and do what the nation chooses, not what he himself chooses. For filling his office in this way, Mr. Lincoln was fitted by the same quality of mental sympathy with the average citizen, which enabled him to reason so convincingly before American audiences; and his natural kindness of heart and rectitude in action were no less correspondent to the character of the nation. He was conscious of the necessity of thus acting, not as an autocrat, but as an agent. Mr. Carpenter says, " Mr. Lincoln liked to feel himself the attorney of the people, not their ruler. Speaking once of the probability of his re-nomination, he said : ' If the people think I have managed their case for them well enough to trust me to carry it on to the next term, I am sure I shall be glad to take it.'" In conversing with Colonel—then Major—Halpine, who suggested a plan to relieve him from great part of the immense number of personal applications and interviews that burdened him so heavily, he expressed more fully the same idea. He said, "For myself, I feel—though the tax on my time is heavy—that no hours of my day are better employed than those which thus bring me again within the direct contact and atmosphere of our whole people." * * * "I tell you, Major, that I call these receptions my 'public-opinion baths;' for I have but little time to read the papers and gather public opinion that way; and though they may not be pleasant in all their particulars, the effect as a whole is renovating and invigorating to my perceptions of responsibility and duty."

PERSONAL APPEARANCE.

. The following description of Mr. Lincoln's person, from an address by his law partner, Mr. Herndon, is almost as original a piece of work as any of Mr. Lincoln's own, and is a very graphic representation of the man:

"He was about six feet four inches high, and when he left this city was fifty-one years old, having good health and no gray hairs, or but few, on his head. He was thin, wiry, sinewy, raw-boned; thin through the breast to the back, and narrow across the shoulders; standing, he leaned forward—was what may be called stoop-shouldered, inclining to the consumptive by build. His usual weight was one hundred and sixty pounds. His organization—rather his structure and functions—worked slowly. His blood had to run a long distance from his heart to the extremities of his frame, and his nerve-force had to travel through dry ground a long distance before his muscles were obedient to his will. His structure was loose and leathery; his body was shrunk and shriveled, having dark skin, dark hair—looking woe-struck. The whole man, body and mind, worked slowly, creakingly, as if it needed oiling. Physically, he was a very powerful man, lifting with ease four hundred or six hundred pounds. His mind was like his body, and worked slowly but strongly. When he walked, he moved cautiously but firmly, his long arms and hands on them, hanging like giant's hands, swung down by his side. He walked with even tread, the inner sides of his feet being parallel. He put the whole foot flat down on the ground at once, not landing on the heel; he likewise lifted his foot all at once, not rising from the toe, and hence he had no spring to his walk. He had economy of fall and lift of foot, though he had no spring or apparent ease of motion in his tread. He walked undulatory, up and down, catching and pocketing tire, weariness, and pain, all up and down his person, preventing them from locating. The first opinion of a stranger, or a man who did not observe closely, was that his walk implied shrewdness, cunning —a tricky man; but his was the walk of caution and firmness. In sitting down on a common chair he was no taller than ordinary men. His legs and arms were, abnormally, unnaturally long, and in undue proportion to the balance of his body. It was only when he stood up that he loomed above other men.

" Mr. Lincoln's head was long and tall from the base of the brain and from the eyebrows. His head ran backward, his forehead rising as it ran back at a low angle, like Clay's, and, unlike Webster's, almost perpendicular. The size of his hat, measured at the hatter's block, was seven and an eighth, his head being, from ear to ear, six and a half inches, and from the front to the back of the brain eight inches. Thus measured, it was not below the medium size. His forehead was narrow but high; his hair was dark, almost black, and lay floating where his fingers or the winds left it, piled up at random. His cheek-bones were high, sharp, and prominent; his eyebrows heavy and prominent; his jaws were long, up-curved, and heavy; his nose was large, long, and blunt, a little awry toward

the right eye; his chin was long, sharp, and up-curved; his
eyebrows cropped out like a huge rock on the brow of a hill;
his face was long, sallow, and cadaverous, shrunk, shriveled,
wrinkled, and dry, having here and there a hair on the surface; his cheeks were leathery; his ears were large, and ran
out almost at right angles from his head, caused partly by
heavy hats and partly by nature; his lower lip was thick, hanging, and under-curved, while his chin reached for the lip up-
curved; his neck was neat and trim, his head being well bal-
anced on it; there was the lone mole on the right cheek, and
Adam's apple on his throat.

"Thus stood, walked, acted, and looked Abraham Lincoln.
He was not a pretty man by any means, nor was he an ugly
one; he was a homely man, careless of his looks, plain-look-
ing and plain-acting. He had no pomp, display, or dignity,
so-called. He appeared simple in his carriage and bearing.
He was a sad-looking man; his melancholy dripped from him
as he walked. His apparent gloom impressed his friends, and
created a sympathy for him—one means of his great success.
He was gloomy, abstracted, and joyous—rather humorous—by
turns. I do not think he knew what real joy was for many
years.

"Mr. Lincoln sometimes walked our streets cheerily—good-
humoredly, perhaps joyously—and then it was, on meeting a
friend, he cried 'How d'y?' clasping one of his friend's hands
in both of his, giving a good hearty soul-welcome. Of a winter's morning, he might be seen stalking and stilting it toward
the market-house, basket on arm, his old gray shawl wrapped
around his neck, his little Willie or Tad running along at his
heels, asking a thousand little quick questions, which his father
heard not, not even then knowing that little Willie or Tad was
there, so abstracted was he. When he thus met a friend, he
said that something put him in mind of a story which he heard
in Indiana or elsewhere, and tell it he would, and there was no
alternative but to listen.

"Thus, I say, stood and walked and looked this singular
man. He was odd, but when that gray eye and face and every
feature were lit up by the inward soul in fires of emotion, *then*

it was that all these apparently ugly features sprang into organs of beauty, or sunk themselves into a sea of inspiration that sometimes flooded his face. Sometimes it appeared to me that Lincoln's soul was just fresh from the presence of its Creator."

Abraham Lincoln was born poor; had scarcely the bare rudiments of education and no money; he lived in the backwoods, and had to do the exhausting and time-consuming manual labor of frontier settlements, in order to live; he had not one single brilliant intellectual trait or faculty to help him; he had neither books, teachers, money, nor time; neither an intellectual home nor the culture of systematic study. Yet toiling to the uttermost, and simply doing his best with unbroken and undiscouraged steadiness, he lived a singularly useful, successful, and even a heroically symmetrical and noble life. He was a good citizen, a most beneficent friend and neighbor, a helper of the needy, only over-kind as a parent, an honest and able lawyer, a powerful and useful public speaker, a shrewd and yet a fair politician, a lover of justice and right, a patient and just and determined and sagacious and far-seeing ruler. His fame is one with the saving of a nation and the redemption of a race; he is one of those very few men whose names can not be forgotten, because his goodness, as well as his office, marks a great epoch in human history.

There is no room here to quote any of the very numerous and enthusiastic praises that friends and foes alike have abundantly bestowed upon Mr. Lincoln. It is the fate of good and bad men alike to be reviled while alive. But it must have been a good man whose memory shines with such bright unspotted splendor of praise as has been awarded to Mr. Lincoln since his death. The rulers of England who did their best to help our nation into ruin under a lying pretense of neutrality; the English newspapers that had ranted and sneered at us and at him all through the war; life-long political opponents, thorough-going rebels, underhand traitors in the North, doubtful or dissatisfied partisans and unqualified supporters, all alike joined in one immense voice of unbroken commendation and mourning when he was taken away. And—what was a far nobler and more desirable possession than all—he had and still has the love and the prayers of the ignorant and oppressed negroes; a voice that makes but small sound on earth, but which comes before the throne of God with a far stronger and loftier tone than that of all the white men who ever lauded him. If the Emancipation of the Slaves was the greatest deed since Christ, assuredly the blessings of the black people are the best blessings that any man has had since Christ.

As one indication—though doubtless an uncertain test—of the extent and depth of Mr. Lincoln's popularity with the American people, it may be mentioned that since his death there has appeared a printed list of three hundred and eighty books, sermons, eulogies, and addresses upon his life or death; and this list is by no means complete.

The lessons of Mr. Lincoln's life are: the power of determined labor and thorough honesty, and the value of character, over and beyond any mere brilliancy or force of intellect; and still more, the justness and soundness of the basis principles of our American liberty. Any European kingdom—say England—will be as good a country as America, when a "hired man" shall by merit become its king. That simple test is typical of the two continents. In no other nation on earth than the United States can good qualities alone, without intrigue or lying, without shedding blood, or privy conspiracy, or levying war, carry a man through so lofty a career.

8

V.

WILLIAM HENRY SEWARD.

SECRETARY SEWARD has during the rebellion had espe-
cial official charge of the foreign relations of the United
States, and has likewise been often an adviser of the
President about home affairs.   Mr. Seward, before being Secretary of State, had been United States Senator
from New York, Governor of New York, and State
Senator.   Besides holding those important offices, he
has been long and widely known as a laborious student,
a good writer, a powerful orator, a shrewd and able
lawyer, a skillful and successful politician and party-
leader, and an enlightened statesman.   Of the Cabinet
of Mr. Lincoln, he was the only one who suggested
any modifications actually adopted as to the Great
Proclamation, and these were important ones.   He advised and secured the insertion of the words "and
maintain" in that paper, where it had at first only said
that it would "recognize" the freedom of the emancipat-
ed slaves.   And he suggested waiting to issue the Proclamation accompanied with victory instead of defeat.

Mr. Seward was born at Florida, Orange County,
New York, May 16, 1801.   He was therefore eight
years older than Mr. Lincoln, and is one year younger
than the century.   His father's ancestors were Welsh,
and those of his mother, Mary Jennings, Irish.   His
grandfather, John Seward, was a Colonel in the Revo-
lutionary army, and an energetic Whig leader in Sus-

sex County, New Jersey, where he lived. The Colonel's son, Samuel S. Seward, father of the Secretary, removed to Florida, New York, in 1795; and during the next twenty years accumulated a considerable fortune by practicing as a physician, and at the same time doing a large mercantile business. After retiring from active employment, he used to lend a good deal of money to farmers in the vicinity, and he never excused any one from paying the legal interest, never would take more than that, and never demanded any of the principal from any one who paid the interest regularly. He was for a long time a holder of public offices, and for seventeen years county judge.

Mary Jennings Seward, the Secretary's mother, was a woman of clear and strong mind, remarkable cheerfulness, a most diligent housewife, and charitable, hospitable, and beneficent. It would be difficult to choose a better parentage; and it is easy to trace in Mr. Seward the influence and the traits of both his parents. His remarkable and unfailing hopefulness and belief in the future is perhaps the most characteristic of all his mental traits; and this he received from his mother. His father had chosen, instead of a portion in money, to receive a liberal education; and this trait of desire for knowledge was reproduced in the son, but greatly intensified. He ran away, not from school, but to it; he was always reading; and when some boys threw stones at him as he was studying while driving the cows home, he was so intent on the book that he merely turned round and walked backward to escape the missiles, still reading away. Coming to a small stream, he missed the bridge, and backed into the water. If an elder brother had not seen him and pulled him out still alive, though unconscious, his career would have ended then and there.

Mr. Seward's whole career has been marked by great aptness to work in and by means of politically organ- ized' forms and associations. This tendency was just about as distinct in him from his ninth to his fifteenth year, while he was at school at Goshen Academy, as when he bore a chief part in organizing and conduct- ing the Whig party, eighteen years afterward. At this academy the boy was a leading member of the " Clas- sical Society" and of the " Goshen Club," and the constitutions and minutes of both of them are mostly in his handwriting. When fifteen, he went to Schen- ectady to be examined for admission into Union Col- lege. He was found qualified for the junior class ; but was advised to enter sophomore because he was so young, and did so.

His college course was successful, as might be ex- pected. He was laborious in the extreme, as he has been, both before and since ; he usually rose at four and worked up all his lessons for the day, and passed the evening in general reading, or studies and compositions for class or society literary exercises or debates, while the other students were doing the routine work that he was going to do next morning before breakfast.

In the last year of his course, an affair occurred which brought out in young Seward with curious accuracy, and a singular-sort of political antetyping, exactly the chief traits that have marked his subsequent career ; an ambition, subordinate to ethical principles ; an ex- treme faith in his own beliefs ; power in setting forth

those beliefs; not an indifference to the judgments of
others, but rather a belief in the justice of the judgments of others when they should have considered the
whole matter; and a strong love and reverence for the
United States as a nation, free, one, and undivided.
The circumstances were these : There were in the college two literary societies, the Adelphic and Philoma-
thean, young Seward being a member of the former.
Some twenty-five Southern students had left Princeton,
come to Union, and joined the Philomatheans. Sec-
tional debates quickly arose, and the vote on them was
against the Southerners, who seceded and formed a
third society. On this state of facts arose a controversy within the Adelphic Society, whether the secession was justifiable. On this controversy Seward, on
returning from an absence South, found himself a sort
of umpire in the society, heard arguments, and decided
that the secession was wrong. This was agreeable to
the freshmen and sophomores of the Adelphic, but
not to his own classmates, the seniors, who caused
a court of inquiry, with the view of expelling him
from the Adelphic. There was a prosecutor, and the
forms of a trial for misdemeanor were observed. Testimony was given, and Seward argued his own cause,
making a strong argument, and following with a spirited review of his own conduct. He closed by avow-
ing with enthusiastic rhetoric that he was indifferent to
what the public prosecutor should say of him, had no
wish to know who voted for or who against him, and
would not embarrass any member either by being present at the vote or by inquiring about it afterward—and
so ending, he went straight out of the room. The re-

sult was a triumphant victory over the prosecution, and a handsome vindication of law and order, and of the principles of the Union.

While still a student, Mr. Seward was chosen to make an address, on behalf of the young Republicans of the college, to Vice-President Tompkins, then visiting Schenectady ; and his speech on this occasion had so little of the student or politician, and so much of the orator and man in it, that it rendered the Vice-President, as long as he lived, a firm and warm friend of the speaker.

At graduation, Seward, against bitter opposition, obtained the highest honor of the day—an appointment by the Adelphic Society as commencement orator. The theme on which he spoke was one which, like the name of the college where he graduated, might be fancied a premonition of many things in the speaker's subsequent career. It was " The Integrity of the American Union." In the same class with Mr. Seward graduated Hon. William Kent, Rev. Dr. L. P. Hickok, the well-known metaphysician, and Rev. Tayler Lewis, who, like Dr. Hickok, is now an officer of the college.

Mr. Seward studied law under John Anthon, of New York city, and worked over his law books as hard as over his class books. As he went through one work after another, he completed and tested his mastery of it by making a written analysis. He afterward studied with Messrs. John Duer and Ogden Hoffman, of Goshen, was admitted to the bar in 1822, and in January, 1823, fixed his residence at Auburn and went into a law partnership with Hon. Elijah Miller, an eminent lawyer and first judge of Cayuga County. During

1824 he married Judge Miller's youngest daughter, Francis Adeline, who died during the rebellion. She was a woman of great excellence and of remarkable breadth of judgment and wisdom in counsel.

During the early years of his residence at Auburn, Mr. Seward gave a good deal of time and labor to militia affairs, and rose to be colonel of a regiment. It is on record that he was "an excellent tactician and an accomplished commander." Doubtless this work was done in part for the sake of extending his acquaintance; a reason which has occasioned the very same step to many a young lawyer, and with like success.

Mr. Seward, as his college career showed, was naturally disposed to politics. His tastes led that way, he had the abilities needed to gratify them, and his pecuniary prospects were not such as to imprison him constantly within mere legal labors. As soon therefore as an occasion arose, he stepped promptly into the political arena, where he has been a strenuous and efficient combatant ever since, and of whose prizes there remains but one for which he need naturally feel any ambition.

The real political question before the United States in those days was the same that has been forever decided by the rebellion. It was, Slavery or Freedom? In February, 1820, the Missouri Compromise had been carried through Congress; and doubtless the graduating oration of young Seward, on "The Integrity of the Union," must have been inspired in theme and in doctrine by the threats and flourishes about disunion and nullification which were flung about so freely in those days by Southern politicians. Mr. Seward's father was

an earnest Jeffersonian Democrat, and, as frequently
happens, the son followed at first in the footsteps of his
parent. But he soon entered another road, and began
with boldness, decision, and foresight, not by joining a
powerful party, but by organizing an apparently feeble
opposition.

This was in October, 1824, when he drafted the address of the Republican Convention of Cayuga County. This address was perhaps the first positive step of
the measures which resulted in the formation of the
Whig party. What it actually did for this purpose
was, to make a public exposition of the history and
principles and practices of that famous political circle
the Albany Regency, thus preparing the way to attack
and break down the power of the Democratic party in
New York, so often the key State of our national
politics.

Within the next three years Mr. Seward on two important occasions set forth in public his chief principles
as a politician, being the same in substance as they still
are. The first of these was a Fourth-of-July Oration,
at Auburn, in which he stated the powers of our national government, claimed that the United States
should be a city of refuge for all that are oppressed,
and insisted with his accustomed zeal and confidence
upon the perpetuity of the Union. The second of these
occasions was during the Greek Revolution, when, in
February, 1827, he addressed at Auburn a meeting to
raise funds to aid the Greeks. This oration was an enthusiastic appeal for liberty everywhere, and for liberal
aid from the United States to those seeking it; and the
result was a most generous contribution.

At twenty-seven years of age, Mr. Seward presided, with great ability and success, over the first political convention of the young men of New York, held at Utica, August 12, 1828. This convention was called in favor of John Quincy Adams as against Andrew Jackson; but the general beat the statesman, and the defeat dissolved the "National Republican" party, at least in Western New York. The abduction of William Morgan, of Batavia, in the autumn of 1826, had meanwhile raised up a furious whirlwind of anti-masonic excitement throughout Western New York, and the political "Anti-Masonic" party was forthwith founded upon it. The issue was, however, not broad enough for a national one. The anti-masons carried all before them in Western New York for some years; once elected a Governor of Pennsylvania; in 1827 polled in New York a vote of 33,000, and two years later of 128,000, but never elected their Governor; did govern Vermont for some years; had a Presidential ticket (the Wirt and Ellmaker ticket) in the field in 1831, which, however, carried no State but Vermont; and in a few years the tariff and currency questions of the Jackson period quite superseded the anti-masonic controversy.

During the existence of the anti-masonic party, which was a sort of bridge between the Republicans and the Whigs, Mr. Seward was adopted by the anti-masons in 1830, as candidate to the State Senate, and was elected by 2,000 majority, though Granger, anti-masonic candidate for Governor, was beaten in the State by 8,000.

The senatorship was followed by the Whig nomination for Governor in 1834, Mr. Seward, however, being defeated by Mr. Marcy. But in 1838 he was elected,

and by a large majority, and in 1840 was re-elected,
declining a third nomination, notwithstanding the earnest efforts of his friends to the contrary. The State
senatorship and the service as Governor constitute Mr.
Seward's career in the administration of State affairs,
and his policy and the measures which he urged, adopted, communicated, or originated give evidence of remarkable wisdom, practical judgment, foresight, and
elevation of view.

At entering the Senate Mr. Seward was not yet
twenty-nine years of age, and was the youngest man
who had ever been chosen to that body. The Legislature, as well as the State, was largely Jacksonian Democratic, and Mr. Seward, who had already inaugurated
the opposition campaign in the country, at once entered into the opposition ranks at the capital, and quickly
became their acknowledged leader. But in conducting
this opposition, as throughout his career in State administration, he sought to accomplish objects intrinsi-
cally good, along with and as a means of, the objects
of party and political success. He was distinctly a
progressive legislator. Thus, he quickly set to work
to abolish imprisonment for debt, to improve the State
prison discipline, to obtain a separate prison for female
convicts, to promote the construction of the Chenango
Canal, and that of the Erie Canal, an enterprise then
struggling hard for life in the midst of political and
money perplexities. His very first speech was as characteristic of his political originality and foresight, as
his conduct of the college society prosecution was of
his faith in himself and independence in thinking. It
was a careful and elaborate argument for an entire

change of the State militia system, urging the plan of volunteer uniform companies instead of the old fashion of obliging every citizen to do military duty. His views were adopted in substance—twenty years afterward.

Of a like wise and liberal spirit was his advocacy of the plan for publishing the well-known Documentary History of the State of New York, which was carried out while he was Governor, though the work was not published until after his term. When the people of New York city asked leave to elect their mayor, instead of having him appointed at Albany, he strongly urged the method by popular vote, for all other cities as well as New York.

Mr. Seward was as young a Governor as he was senator and student, being but thirty-seven when elected. He was only thirty-three when first nominated. This youthfulness was strenuously urged against him, but to little purpose; for the election carried him into the Governor's chair by a strong majority, and gave the Whig party—then but six years old—full control of the Empire State. During his service as Governor, Mr. Seward upheld in word and deed the measures and doctrines of the Whig party. But with large wisdom, he also strove to join with those measures a readiness to adopt and perfect any improvement or scheme whatever within the scope of government and calculated to do good. To establish a reputation for doing this must necessarily be a far more permanent kind of party capital than to be exclusively identified with some one measure or set of measures, whose definite victory or defeat must in either event end the existence of the party whose life they were. Thus he prompted the establishment of the normal school system, according to the best lights of the day, and advocated that sound modern doctrine, that the state needs to enforce the education of *all* children. With judicious distinction between true religion and religious intolerance, he favored the employment of Roman Catholic teachers for the children of those who would have no other. He urged, and at length saw adopted, the abolition of the special disabilities long inflicted on foreign-born citizens ; and when the mayor of New York city advised a tax on immigrants, with the idea of keeping them out and thus avoiding some of the poverty and crime which they brought with them, he met this short-sighted proposition with a strong and clear explanation of the great value of the foreign laborer in developing the resources of our new country. Governor Seward clearly understood what the great French political philosopher De Tocqueville saw so clearly, that the free institutions of the United States find one main security in the multiplication of centers of political power, as distinguished from the French or rather European or monarchical practice of centralizing that power wholly in the hands of the supreme government. Accordingly, he labored to secure the election of judges by the people, instead of the previous method, which gave the State judicial appointments either directly to the Governor or indirectly to the managers of the prevailing party, whichever that might be.

Governor Seward was a firm, vigorous, and efficient friend of the Erie Canal, and stood by the great enterprise through good report and evil, until it was at last completed. It is an odd circumstance, as he related himself in a speech on the completion of the Erie Railroad, that he wrote what he thought the *chef-d'œuvre* of his college life, in the form of an argument to show that either the canal could never be completed, or if it should be it would ruin the State. The spirit of this production is very natural for a wise boy as contrasted with a wise man, but the boy's argument is of exactly the same intellectual character with the man's, in its forecasting, its earnest effort to judge of the future. He was as good a friend of railroads as of canals; materially aided in the completion of the Erie Railroad, as subsequently in the United States Senate he advocated the Pacific Railroad. Interest in such great industrial enterprises is however to be credited to higher and deeper views than those of party politics. It depends not on notions of what is best for a party, but of what is best for the community.

Several critical affairs of public or international interest during Governor Seward's two terms tested his firmness and wisdom, and he stood the test very well. One of these was the " anti-rent trouble," which afterward broke out into what was called the " Helderberg War." The substance of this was an attempt, by the heirs of Stephen Van Rensselaer, Patroon of the manor of Rensselaerwyck, to collect the arrears of rent on certain perpetual leases of manorial lands. As the manor was fifty miles square, the territory and population interested were enough to make quite a disturbance, the tenants resisting with violence and arms any attempts to collect the rents. Governor Seward, to begin with, issued a proclamation requiring submission

to the laws and application to the Legislature for any
required relief, and at the same time a sufficient military force was sent with the sheriff, to enable him to
serve process. Gov. Seward, in his annual message for
1840, recommended a commission to effect a compromise.
Such a one was accordingly accepted by the tenants,
but the landlords unwisely refused it, and the result has
been some insurrectionary troubles, a persistent political agitation, and an immense number of lawsuits, the
whole business ending in the gradual extinction of the
feudal-tenure leases to the footing of ordinary freeholds.
The landlords have thus been driven, with much vexa-
tion and large expense, to just about the position where
Governor Seward's suggestions would have placed them
amicably a quarter of a century ago.

Another and even more troublesome affair was the
famous M'Leod case. M'Leod, a Canadian, having
boasted, while in Niagara County, N. Y., that he had
helped burn the steamer Caroline, on the night of
December 29, 1837, during the so-called "Patriot War,"
was at once seized and held for trial on a charge of
arson. The British minister protested, claiming that
the burning was an act of war, and that M'Leod was
therefore not liable to civil trial. President Van Buren
however decided that the act was a civil crime, of which
the New York courts had jurisdiction. In reply, the
British minister, after the manner of his nation, threatened hostilities if M'Leod was not given up; and General Harrison, on succeeding Mr. Van Buren, in substance reversed his predecessor's opinion, and urged
that a *nolle* should be entered in the State court in the
case. Thus Great Britain and the United States were

both against New York; but Mr. Seward quietly caused M'Leod to be tried in regular course of law. He was acquitted; and then, and not before, Governor Seward had him sent under escort into Canadian territory. The British did not fulfill any of their threats.

At the end of his term, Governor Seward resigned his chair to his successor, Governor Bouck, whom he introduced in form and with kindly courtesy to the people of Albany—a wise and good-natured deed, never before done in the State. One week after leaving the governorship he was hard at work in his law office in Auburn, and he at once resumed and largely increased a profitable business in the State courts. This was in a year or two somewhat modified, as his talent for managing patent cases soon brought him a large practice in the United States courts. During the six years between the governorship and his election to the United States Senate in February, 1849, besides his large law business, he was constantly consulted by the Whig leaders, and was an efficient laborer in aid of that party during the Presidential campaigns of 1844 and 1848. He was elected United States senator by a vote of 121 to 30.

Mr. Seward's senatorial career lasted twelve years, including the administrations of Presidents Taylor, Fillmore, Pierce, and Buchanan; and covered that historically important period during which the North and South were verging toward the two opposite attitudes on the moral-political question of slavery, which resulted in the rebellion. During all this period Mr. Seward was a powerful and steadfast champion, according to his own views of expediency and right, of the anti-slavery extension sentiments of the North. While President Taylor lived, Mr. Seward was one of his closest friends and counselors. At the instant of his reaching Washington, he found the principle of slavery involved in a money bill then before the Senate, to which. Mr. Walker, of Mississippi, had proposed an amendment that would annul in the Mexican territories, just acquired, the Mexican laws prohibiting slavery. The Senate adopted the amendment; but Mr. Seward, without losing a moment, set to work to secure its defeat in the House. After a long and violent debate the House rejected it, and the Senate receded, on the very last night of the session. The next crisis in the great contest was the struggle over the admission of California, and it was in his speech on this question, March 11, 1850, that Mr. Seward used that phrase "The Higher Law," which has since been so often repeated in praise and blame. This famous term was used in arguing that while the Constitution " devotes the national domain to union, to justice, to defense, to welfare, and to liberty," " there is a higher law than the Constitution, which regulates our authority over that domain, *and devotes it to the same noble purposes.*" The term was thus used in proving the agreement of the law of God with the Constitution of the United States; and it is difficult now to see what fault could be found with it.

Whenever the question of human freedom arose, Mr. Seward labored and voted in its favor. He was a consistent and vigorous opponent of the fugitive slave bill, of the pro-slavery element in Mr. Clay's " compromise," and of all those successive victories of slavery which culminated in the repeal of the Missouri Compromise, the Kansas iniquities, the Dred Scott decision, and which worked their own defeat through the reaction which they caused in the North. As in his youth he had argued in favor of the Greeks in their strife against Turkey, so now he spoke earnestly in favor of the Hungarians. Upon questions affecting the industrial and social interests of the United States, Mr. Seward's course in the Senate was substantially a continuation of that which he pursued while legislator and Governor in New York.

As senator, he was remarkably successful in continuing on good terms personally with the imperious and unscrupulous Southern politicians, whose plans he was opposing with all his might. He was, it is true, sometimes treated with discourtesy. One violent fellow proposed to expel him for words used in debate on the fugitive slave bill, and to this threat he replied in his place with dignity and force, quietly defying the threat, and agreeing that on the trial of the question he would use no defense except the very speeches for which the expulsion was threatened. Of course the threat was not fulfilled; the gag-law day was twenty years before.

In 1858, in an election speech at Rochester, Mr. Seward furnished to cotemporary English a second phrase, which has perhaps been more repeated even than "Higher Law." This was "Irrepressible Conflict." The words were used in speaking of the collisions between slave and free labor in the United States, in the following sentences:

"Shall I tell you what this collision means? They who think it is accidental, unnecessary, the work of interested or fanatical agitators, and therefore ephemeral, mistake the case altogether. It is an *irrepressible conflict* between opposing and enduring forces, and it means that the United States must and will, sooner or later, become either entirely a slave-holding nation, or entirely a free-labor nation." This was exactly the substance of what Mr. Lincoln said in his great speech at Springfield, Illinois, in the same summer: "I believe this Government can not endure permanently half slave and half free," etc. But Mr. Lincoln was not then a man of first-class national reputation, and he did not put his thought into a neat phrase. In 1856 as well as in 1861 Mr. Seward was preferred by many Republicans as candidate for the Presidency, and on the first ballot at Chicago in 1860 he received 173 votes to Mr. Lincoln's 103. During both those campaigns, Mr. Seward in good faith and effectively supported his party and its candidates, and Mr. Lincoln, upon election, at once offered to his late competitor the place of Secretary of State. This office has given to Mr. Seward a very influential part in managing the foreign affairs of the United States during the difficult and dangerous period of the rebellion. His performance of this duty—as indeed has been the case with most or all his previous public labors—has been highly praised and deeply blamed. But whether his views have always been correct or not, the fact remains, that while the governments of Europe were ardently desirous of the destruction of this republic, yet no foreign war came upon us while hampered by the rebellion; and that it is certainly doubtful what the issue would have been had the contrary taken place. Of both President.

Lincoln and President Johnson, Mr. Seward has been a most constant and trusted adviser. During Mr. Lincoln's visit to Richmond, Mr. Seward was thrown from a carriage, and his arm and jaw were broken. He was still confined to his bed when the President returned, and making his first visit to the Secretary, he threw himself down across the foot of his bed, and resting his head on one hand, joyfully told the story of his trip and of the entire success of Grant, ending with the words, "and now for a day of thanksgiving!" The Secretary advised, however, to wait until Sherman was heard from, to which Mr. Lincoln agreed, though with reluctance. Mr. Seward, in speaking of his own and Mr. Lincoln's agreement as to government measures, remarked to a friend, "No knife was ever sharp enough to divide us upon any question of public policy, though we frequently arrived at the same conclusion through different processes of thought. Once only did we disagree in sentiment." When asked on what occasion, the answer was, "His ' colonization' scheme; which I opposed on the self-evident principle that all natives of a country have an equal right to the soil."

Mr. Seward was made a victim of the same conspiracy which assassinated Mr. Lincoln. While confined helpless to his bed by the injuries received from his fall, he was attacked by a powerful young man named Lewis Payne Powell, and fearfully stabbed and cut; and only very wonderful vigor of constitution and tenacity of life could have enabled him to recover so completely from injuries so serious. Mr. Carpenter's account of the way in which Mr. Seward detected the fact of the President's death, which his attendants had been carefully concealing from him, is striking. He says:

"The Sunday following, he had his bed wheeled around so that he could see the tops of the trees in the park opposite his residence—just putting on their spring foliage—when his eyes caught sight of the Stars and Stripes at half-mast on the War Department, on which he gazed awhile, then turning to his attendant said: 'The President is dead!' The confused attendant stammered as he tried to say nay; but the Secretary could not be deceived. 'If he had been alive, he would have been the first to call on me,' he continued; 'but he has not been here, nor has he sent to know how I am; and there is the flag at half-mast.' The statesman's inductive reason had discerned the truth, and in silence the great tears coursed down his gashed cheeks. as it sank into his heart."

Perhaps the chief points in Mr. Seward's character may be summed thus: In politics, he is a shrewd, practical manager; in statesmanship, he is hopeful, liberal, utilitarian, and far-sighted; in mind, he is always chiefly a reasoner though also a rhetorician, and a reasoner from first principles, with a peculiar tendency to forecasting. Besides these chief traits, he is very industrious, independent, self-reliant, and benevolent. There have also been indications of the same desire in him for a high future fame, which many great men of ancient times possessed, and which grows rare in these days. It is said that his life-long opposition to slavery was first brought into vivid activity by an incident at the South, where he passed a portion of his senior college year as a teacher. He was traveling, it appears, on horseback, and found a slave woman, with a miserable old blind horse and a bag of corn, on her way to mill, but afraid to try to cross a broken-down bridge. In trying to help her over, the old horse fell partly through the bridge and stuck fast. The young man was unable to get him out, and so he mounted his own horse, rode to the house of the master of the slave, and told him the story, seeking to excuse the slave. But the planter replied with a monstrous bombardment of curses on himself, the slave, the horse, the bridge, and pretty much everything and everybody. The whole affair so deeply disgusted him that the impression was never forgotten.

Besides his political career and his labors as a lawyer, Mr. Seward has shown decided ability as a business man, and in literature. In the former capacity he acted for the year or two about 1836 when he served as agent to settle the complicated and confused affairs of the Holland Land Company, which he adjusted with great tact and judgment. His literary productions, the occasional hasty work of scanty leisure, include a number of addresses on anniversary and society occasions, obituary orations on John Quincy Adams, Daniel O'Connell, Lafayette, Henry Clay, Daniel Webster, and others— a published biography of John Quincy Adams, and the historical introduction to the great State "Natural History of New York."

A good instance of the effectiveness of Mr. Seward's mode of arguing from general principles to particular cases occurred in the New York Court of Errors about 1834. This court was the court of final appeal in the State, and consisted of the chancellor, the judges of the

Supreme Court, and the members of the State Senate. Mr. Seward was the youngest member of this court, but a diligent, laborious, and useful member. On the occasion referred to—the case of Parks *vs.* Jackson, the appeal was from the Supreme Court, where a technical legal rule had been so applied as to take away from certain parties estates which they had honestly bought and paid for. According to the forms of the Court of Errors, Judge Nelson, now of the United States Supreme Court, then of the State Supreme Court, stated the reasons for the decision of his court. Then Chancellor Walworth delivered an opinion, in which he defended the decision. Mr. Seward now rose, and made an argument on the contrary part, in which he urged the claims of substantial justice as higher than those of an arbitrary legal rule. The question was taken on reversing the judgment. The judges of the court appealed from did not vote; but except Chancellor Walworth, who abode by his technics, every vote was given in favor of the reversal which Mr. Seward demanded.

A curious and characteristic specimen of Mr. Seward's methods of thought when applied out of place, and of his thorough confidence in the correctness of his own views, is given in his criticism upon Mr. Carpenter's great commemorative picture. He rather abruptly said to the artist one evening, "I told the President the other day that you were painting your picture on a false presumption." The artist, surprised, asked why. The Secretary explained, that it was the election of Mr. Lincoln, not the proclamation, which was the death-knell of slavery; that the business of Mr. Lincoln's administration was not abolition, but the salvation of the nation; and, he continued, "Had you consulted me for a subject to paint, I should not have given you the Cabinet Council on Emancipation, but the meeting which took place when the news came of the attack upon Sumter, when the first measures were organized for the restoration of the national authority. *That* was the crisis in the history of this administration —not the issue of the Emancipation Proclamation." And referring again to the comparative unimportance of the slavery question, he continued: "If I am to be remembered by posterity, let it not be as having loved predominantly white men or black men, but as one who loved his country." Mr. Carpenter argued to the contrary, but the Secretary stuck to his opinion. "Well," he said, "you may think so, and this generation may agree with you, but posterity will hold a different opinion." It may be added, that the picture of Mr. Buchanan in the corner, white with terror, and with a stump of a cigar between his teeth, with his Cabinet quarreling so hard that he had to turn them all out, according to Mr. Stanton's description, would have been a strange subject to adopt as the characteristic scene of the war. In this preference Mr. Seward was wrong. His reasoning as a statesman may have been correct enough in one sense, but the chief cause or occasion of a circumstance is not necessarily the best artistic representation of its spirit; and Mr. Carpenter certainly judged justly as an artist.

The position and attitude of Mr. Seward in Mr. Carpenter's picture are prominent and characteristic. The Secretary of State is by etiquette the senior member of the Cabinet; Mr. Seward was, moreover, by virtue of his abilities, attainments, and principles, a chief adviser with the President, unofficially. So he sits at the front of the table, his hand rested upon it in an argumentative posture, with fore-finger, as it were, distinguishing the exact point to be made. The face expresses steady sense and calm thought, as the Secretary advises to wait for military success before the issuing of the Proclamation, instead of putting it forth upon the heels of disaster.

VI.

S. P. CHASE.

Salmon Portland Chase now Chief-Justice of the United States, was born in Cornish, New Hampshire, January 13, 1808. His father was a farmer, and the country was so unsettled, schools so scarce, and books so costly, that when at three years of age it was time for the boy to learn his letters, they were set down for him on smooth pieces of birch-bark.

The name of Chase is somewhat widely spread in New Hampshire and Vermont. It is said that it was of the family to which the Chief-Justice belongs, that the saying was first uttered which has since, with a difference, been applied to Dr. Lyman Beecher. The story is that some one said of an old yellow house in Cornish, long the Chase homestead, that in it had been born more brains than in any other house in New England. Philander Chase, the eminent pioneer Episcopal bishop of Ohio, was the Chief-Justice's uncle; and so was Dudley Chase, at one time United States senator from Vermont. Another uncle, Salmon, a lawyer in Portland, had died there, and after him and the city the Chief-Justice was named. The men of the Chase family are tall, strong, large-framed, large-headed, decided, energetic, and progressive men, and the Chief-Justice does no discredit to his kinsmen, either in physique or in mind and will.

In 1815, his father, Ithamar Chase, removed to Keene, to superintend a glass factory there in which he was largely interested; but three years afterward died suddenly, probably by a sun-stroke. His affairs were at the time much deranged in consequence of the ruinous competition of English glass with the products of his factory; and the widow, upon the settlement of the estate, was able to retain nothing, either from the factory, or from a tavern, or a farm which the energetic man had carried on at the same time with reasonable success. But Mrs. Chase had much of the prudence and force of character of her own Scottish ancestry, and having a small property of her own, she removed to a little cottage in the neighborhood and set to work with good courage and full faith to bring up her children. Salmon, with one of his sisters, a little afterward spent some time at a boarding-school, in Windsor, Vt., where he made a good beginning in Latin, and where he partook in an odd style of chastisement, invented apparently by the Yankee principal. This gentleman, when the boys were noisy at night and awoke him, used to come noiselessly up to their door, burst in, drag them all out of bed by the hair into a pile in the middle of the floor, and disappear to allow them to digest his hint. One of the youths shaved his hair close to elude the teacher's hand; but only to discover that portions of the human frame, very distant from the head, could also be made to suffer pain.

In 1820, Bishop Chase offered to take charge of the boy in Ohio and give him an education, and with an elder brother on the way to join the expedition of General Cass to the upper Mississippi, and with Mr. Schoolcraft, geologist to the same expedition, he went West. The party stopped at Buffalo, and Alexander Chase and Mr. Schoolcraft made a two days' visit to Niagara, leaving the boy behind as too young. He was, however, quite as curious and enterprising as he was young; and finding at the tavern a companion of his own age equally desirous to see the Falls, the two little fellows walked through the snow twenty miles to Niagara, saw the sight, found their surprised seniors, and returned with them. At Cleveland Salmon stopped, to proceed to Worthington, Ohio, the other two going on to Detroit. As he could not go alone through the woods, he had to wait some weeks for convoy at Cleveland, and turned the time to account by running a sort of *extempore* ferry across the Cuyahoga. This was in order to pay his board with his entertainer; but that gentleman, a warm admirer of Bishop Chase, refused to accept the money.

At Worthington young Chase remained about two years, and had a reasonably severe experience. His uncle the bishop was a somewhat absolute person and stern in his manner. He was poor besides; for in Ohio in those days money was so scarce, transportation so dear, produce so cheap, and postage so high, that it took a bushel of wheat to pay the postage on a letter, and the bishop used to say that all the revenues of his bishopric would not pay his postage bill. So he kept a school, by means of an assistant, and carried on a farm, as unavoidable means for supporting himself. Salmon, therefore, not being a boarder like the other boys, but a member of the family, had to work as the family did, "doing chores" and all sorts of

farm labor, and learning and reciting his lessons in such
other time as he could command. He toiled resolutely
through everything, however, and stood well in his
classes. He was quite near-sighted, which was an additional obstacle; and he lisped considerably, besides;
but he got rid of this last difficulty by pursuing for a
number of months a course of reading aloud for the
purpose. Notwithstanding the arbitrary and severe
ways of Bishop Chase, he seems to have discerned the
good qualities of his nephew; for one day, when the
youth asked leave to go in swimming with some other
boys, the bishop refused, saying, " Why, Salmon, the
country might lose its future President if you should
get drowned!"

In the autumn of 1822 Bishop Chase removed to
Cincinnati to take charge of a college there, and took
his nephew with him. The youth entered freshman, but
worked rapidly ahead of the regular course by reciting
privately to a fellow-student, so that he was soon able
to be examined for and enter into the sophomore class.

When in 1823 Bishop Chase left Cincinnati for that
journey to Europe in which he collected the means of
founding Kenyon College, young Chase had to leave
too, and coming East with the bishop and his family,
he returned home to Keene, intending to enter and
graduate at Dartmouth. After an unsuccessful experiment at teaching district school, he passed the winter
at home in study; during the following summer passed
a short time at the academy at Royalton, Vt., and then
entered junior at Dartmouth.

Here he worked as hard as ever, and graduated eighth
in rank. He was in those days occasionally somewhat

absent-minded, and once, pulling off his trowsers, with some vague notion of toilet management, and beating them over a chair to get the dust out, pounded to pieces his watch, which he left in the fob. A rather more creditable occurrence during his college days at Dartmouth, showed the same quick and strong sense of justice and indignation at wrong which has always been a prominent trait in his character. A class-mate was sent away from college by the faculty for some transgression of which he was not guilty, having been given, after the fashion of faculty tribunals, twenty-four hours in which to confess what he did not do, and having been refused permission to see his accuser. Young Chase hereupon remonstrated with the president, but without avail, and he therefore coolly told the dignitary that he would also leave, as he did not wish to remain where his friends were liable to such injustice. They went together, accordingly, their class-mates agreeing in regret for the injustice of the action. But they had not driven fairly out of sight in their old gig, before a student rode after them to notify them that the sentence was reconsidered and that they might return. They, however, observed that they must have a few days in which to see if they would reconsider; and taking a week's vacation, they went back.

In the autumn of 1826 the young man went to Washington, where his uncle, Dudley Chase, was senator from Vermont. His intention was to set up a private school, but having advertised and waited in vain until his last dollar was gone, he asked his uncle to obtain him a place under the Government. The senator, however, replied that he had once obtained an appointment for

a nephew, and it ruined him. And he added, "If you
want half a dollar to buy a spade and go out and
dig for a living, I'll give it to you cheerfully; but I
will not get you a place under Government." The discouraged youth departed, and waited some time longer,
until by good fortune a certain Mr. Plumley made over
to him his classical school, already established and profitable. This was in consequence of the still greater success of a girls' school which Mrs. Plumley had opened,
and which required the labor of both. Many years
afterward, Mr. Chase, when Secretary of the Treasury,
had the pleasure of returning Mr. Plumley's kindness
when a return was needed, by giving him a good position in the Treasury Department.

Mr. Chase continued his school until the end of 1839.
During this period he decided to study law, having
been hitherto uncertain whether not to become a clergyman. He now, however, entered the office of William
Wirt as a student, and became also a visitor at his
house. From the savings of his income, now quite a
good one for him, he had the pleasure of repaying to
his mother the money she had advanced him, and of
securing to one of his sisters a good education. A curious occurrence during this same period also seemed
to mark a great change in his health and personal appearance. He had always been slender, pale, and
stooping, and this latter defect he set about trying to
remedy. As he stood one morning stretching himself
up straight by the fire, all at once a sensation of faint-
ness came over him and something in his side seemed
to give way and sink down. A physician told him that
this was the breaking of some inward adhesion conse-

quent upon his habit of stooping, and that its rupture was a good thing. The young man now arranged his desk and organized a set of-exercises, to correct his stoop. He succeeded entirely, and from that time he grew straight and strong, until he acquired the erect and massive dignity of person which has been so conspicuous in his manhood.

In February, 1830, the young law-student passed his examination for admission to the bar, and at its close was recommended to read another year. But he answered that that was inconsistent with his plans, as he had made all his arrangements to go into practice at Cincinnati.

" To Cincinnati ?" said the examining judge, as much as to say, " You know enough for that !" and continued, with a smile, " Mr. Clerk, swear in Mr. Chase."

The young lawyer went to Cincinnati, then a rapidly growing place of about 25,000 inhabitants, and opened his office accordingly. His early experience here as a lawyer was much like that of the outset of his career as a teacher at Washington. For a long time he had absolutely no business except drawing one agreement for a chance customer who paid him half a dollar, and about a week afterward came and borrowed it back! When reduced almost to despair, however, as in Washington, he had the good fortune to find a friend, a Mr. John Young, who loaned him without security " all the money he wanted." After a long time a little business came in. His employers found him faithful and competent, and were pretty sure to come back to him. Having once fairly started, his legal career was one of steady and increasing success, and was marked by

many occurrences of interest. In his very first case of
any importance the judge charged directly against him,
but the jury found in his favor. In the next case he
attacked and broke down together the testimony and
the character of a notoriously violent fellow, an important witness against him, who threatened to have his
blood. Mr. Chase's friends begged him to arm himself, but he declined, and the fellow at the close of the
court put himself in the lawyer's way with the evident
intention of assaulting him. But so calm and stern
was the lawyer's face that the rowdy's heart failed him,
and he walked off.

In 1834 Mr. Chase went to Columbus to make his
first argument before a United States court. On rising
to speak, he was so much agitated by apprehensions
about what was to him a matter of so much importance,
that he could not utter a single sentence. He sat down,
and recovering himself, and in a great rage at himself
for his failure, he rose again in a few moments, delivered his argument, and then sat down again, still in deep
mortification at his false start. It was therefore with
surprise that he saw one of the judges come and shake
his hand, saying, smilingly, " I congratulate you most
sincerely !"

" On what, sir ?" asked the puzzled lawyer.

" On your failure," said the judge. " A person of
ordinary temperament and abilities would have gone
through his part without any such symptoms of nerv-
ousness. But when I see a young man break down
once or twice in that way, I conceive the highest hopes
of him."

In this same year Mr. Chase married and established

in Cincinnati a home of his own, and has ever since been a resident of that city except when at Washington. During, or before these earliest years of his prosperity, Mr. Chase compiled a very thorough edition of the Ohio statutes in three octavo volumes, with full notes and an introductory history of the State. As no complete edition had before been published, the work was a very great assistance to the legal profession, and quickly became the standard edition, recognized as authority in all the courts. This work was in itself of small direct pecuniary profit, but it materially advanced the author's reputation. He soon became solicitor of the United States Bank at Cincinnati, and also of one of the city banks, and rose into a very good practice.

Those who become senators of the United States have to prepare the way for election to that body by becoming influential in the politics of their State. Mr. Chase's public career from about 1836, the date of the Cincinnati mob which destroyed Mr. Birney's abolitionist newspaper, the *Philanthropist*, brought him into such a position. The road which he followed was that successively of abolitionist lawyer, Liberty party man, Free-soiler, and Republican, and in this road he not only gratified his intense love of justice and human right, and his intense hatred of wrong and oppression, but, as it happened, represented and led from the first a very considerable and increasing number of the voters of Ohio. This State was so largely settled from New England, and imbued with New England morals, that it adopted early the anti-slavery tenets of the best Eastern minds. More than this—it is always found that good things from the East grow large and strong

10

when they are transplanted to the West, like trees transferred to a richer and deeper soil; and thus Ohio quickly became the strongest anti-slavery State in the Union, except, perhaps, Massachusetts.

On the occasion of the mob before mentioned, their noise had attracted Mr. Chase's attention, and he had gone into the streets to see the proceedings. While they confined themselves to a forcible entry into Mr. Birney's printing-office, and the destruction of his presses, type, paper, and other stock, he did not interfere. But when he heard them threatening to seize Mr. Birney himself, he hastened by another road round to the hotel where Mr. Birney was living, and quietly stood in the doorway when they came up. As the foremost would have forced a way in, he ordered them back, and argued with them at the same time against either assaulting him or injuring the premises. He thus delayed them some time, until just as they were getting so impatient as to be apparently on the point of making a rush, a well-known citizen appeared and assured the crowd that Mr. Birney was certainly nowhere in the house, and they went disappointed away. It was true. He had escaped while Mr. Chase singly held back the mob, very probably saving the life of the "abolitionist."

Almost immediately after this, Mr. Chase began a noble series of unpaid defenses of colored persons seized as fugitive slaves. This he did against a tremendously bitter and angry public opinion, against the perfectly open pre-judgments of the courts, and out of devotion to justice and to the cause of the oppressed. The first of these cases was that of the slave-girl Matilda, seized in

Cincinnati as a fugitive slave in 1837, in whose defense Mr. Chase argued on *habeas corpus* before the Court of Common Pleas. The defense failed, and the girl was surrendered to her owner and carried back. As Mr. Chase went out of the court-room, a certain conservative and respectable citizen observed, "There goes a promising young man who has just ruined himself." But not only was this series of defenses a principal reason in general for Mr. Chase's influence and popularity with the Free-soil party and the Republican party, but this very case, where the wiseacre thought him "ruined," was a direct and important cause of his election to the United States Senate. There happened to be present during this argument a young medical student named Townsend, who was afterward, in 1848, a member of the Legislature, and was an earnest advocate of Mr. Chase's election. As belonging to neither party, he had much influence with the more liberal of the Democrats, and with a few more of the same opinions he succeeded in repealing a disgraceful code of "Black Laws" then in force in Ohio, and in securing Mr. Chase's election.

In 1842 came up the famous Van Zandt case. Van Zandt, who was the original of Van Tromp in Mrs. Stowe's novel of "Uncle Tom's Cabin," had been sued for damages for carrying off certain fugitive slaves. He did not know them to be such, however, though he may have suspected it. - Mr. Chase's argument in defense of Van Zandt was a wonderfully powerful and convincing argument. It seemed to entirely convince court, jury, and spectators, and the slaveholding plaintiff himself, under the influence of this eloquent plea for human rights, came to Mr. Chase, acknowledged that he was in the wrong, said he did not doubt that he had lost his case, and that he was sorry for having brought the action. So the plaintiff, as well as everybody else, was astounded when the jury gave him a verdict. A second suit was brought against Van Zandt, for a penalty for having "harbored and concealed" fugitives, and this was carried up to the Supreme Court at Washington by the defense. Mr. Chase and Mr. Seward argued it, without compensation; but that court, then, and long afterward, the strongest citadel of the slave power, confirmed the decision of the courts below, and Van Zandt had to pay the money. These two losses pretty much ruined him; but he is not known to have regretted the action for which he suffered.

In the Watson case, the Rosetta case, the Parish case, and other well-known fugitive-slave cases occurring during the period from 1845 to 1856, Mr. Chase served with unfailing ardor the cause of freedom. The prevailing pro-slavery opinions of the community and the courts alike rendered this work futile so far as concerned the wretched negroes who were regularly thrust back into the pit they had struggled out of. But the labor was done for the sake of the principle involved; and no such series of efforts can be made on the right side without causing a gradual change in public sentiment. This change, proceeding in Ohio as in the whole North, was largely caused by Mr. Chase's powerful and fearless advocacy of the helpless and penniless victims that he could not save, and at the earliest possible moment he took care to organize his friends into one of those

party machines which, in the United States, must be
set up before a political principle can be embodied in
the laws. Mr. Chase has been called "the Father of
the Republican party." He was at any rate one of the
earliest and chiefest of those who formed the "Liberty
party," and who rose with it as it expanded into the
"Free-soil party," and then into the "Republican
party." In 1841 he assembled a small meeting at Cincinnati and addressed it, in explanation of the doctrines on which a party for freedom could be organized,
and he then went on to issue a call for a convention of
those opposed to the extension of slavery at Columbus.
This was a line of political action so unpopular that
the newspaper editors—who have a pretty keen scent
for such qualities—would not publish his call, and he
had to pay for it as an advertisement. But the convention met, issued an address written by Mr. Chase,
and organized the Liberty party.

He was now a political leader, and from this time
forward he gave whatever of his life could be spared
from his business to the service of the new party. In
1843 he assisted at the National Liberty Convention
at Buffalo; in 1845 he was the chief means of gather-
ing a "Southern and Western Liberty Convention" at
Cincinnati. He was prominent at the Free Territory
State Convention of Ohio in 1848, and was chairman
of the Buffalo Convention of that year. Mr. Birney
was the first anti-slavery candidate for President. In
1840, he had received about 7,000 votes, scattering and
spontaneous testimonials rather than from an organized
effort. In 1844 he received about 62,700—enough, it
was considered, to reduce Mr. Clay's vote and give the

Presidency to Mr. Polk ; and most furious was the anger of the Whigs against what they considered the unjust and wicked trick. Of course, when so many voters began to declare for any principle, the regular party leaders could begin to see that the principle might be correct, and the Ohio Democratic State Convention took distinct ground against slavery extension. Upon this, Mr. Chase joined himself politically with that party, giving them at the same time notice that he should leave them when they left that ground. He did as he had said in 1852, on their accepting the Pierce platform.

It was by a coalition between the Democrats and Free-soilers of Ohio, greatly promoted, as we have already described, by Dr. Townsend, that Mr. Chase was elected United States senator, February 22d, 1849, and returned as an influential ruler of the land, to the city which he had left nineteen years before, an obscure and unfledged lawyer. He entered the Senate at the same time with Mr. Seward, and his labors as a statesman, like Mr. Seward's, were devoted to the cause of freedom. With the same powerful indignation against injustice that had impelled him in the Ohio fugitive-slave cases, he fought the advance of the slave power, and also with the same apparent certainty of defeat; for the compromise measures of 1850, and the repeal of the Missouri Compromise in 1854, seemed at the time to be. permanent gains for slavery.

As his senatorial term grew toward a close, the Republican party had risen into existence, developing from the Free-soil party as that had grown from the Liberty party. The new party in 1855 nominated and elected him Governor of Ohio, in which office he served for two consecutive terms, with great dignity, judgment, energy, and consistency to his principles. During the first of these terms, in 1856, he declined to become a candidate for the Presidential nomination, although urged by many influential friends. It was in 1856, also, that the Garner case occurred at Cincinati, made horribly famous by the frantic conduct of Margaret Garner, who, finding herself about to be captured by the slave-hunters, snatched up a butcher-knife, declared that she would kill all her children before they should be carried back, and did actually kill one poor little girl three years old. Margaret, her husband, and the rest of the party of fugitives, were secured by State officers, and would probably have escaped had not some rapid legal hocus-pocus and connivance at Cincinnati hurried them out of State custody into that of a slave-hunting United States marshal, who thrust them into an omnibus, guarded them with a force of five hundred special deputies, and ran them off over the river into Kentucky, while Governor Chase was at . Columbus at the annual session of the Legislature. They disappeared into slavery, and have never been heard of since.

In the next year some Kentucky deputy marshals went on a regular slave-hunt into Ohio, where they resisted the State authority, fired on the sheriff of Champaign County, escaped into Green County, resisted and fired on the sheriff of that county also, but finally had to surrender and go to jail at Xenia. They, however, were quickly released on *habeas corpus* by Judge Leavitt, of Cincinnati, the same person who had so swiftly sent off the miserable Garners into slavery. This Green County case was violently asserted, by the political party opposed to Governor Chase, to be an actual armed attack by him or his friends upon the United States Government. This absurd charge did no harm. Indeed, the occurrences themselves were indirectly of vast benefit to the cause of freedom, though so inauspicious in themselves. The result of such decisions as those of this Judge Leavitt was, to assert that a State could not execute its civil or criminal process if such execution interfered with the doings of claimants under the Fugitive Slave Law. As no such claim was set up in any other case, the distinction was so invidious and so very discreditable, that it did much to make that law odious to the public, and to prepare for the overthrow of slavery.

Mr. Chase, who had been again elected to the United States Senate, was a member of that "Peace Convention" which met in Washington in consequence of the invitation of Virginia, given in February, 1860. In this convention he was perfectly willing to assure the revolting States of what they already knew very well —that their rights were not going to be invaded—but he was firm in the conviction that they ought at the same time to be notified that slavery would not be allowed any further extension. The convention could not, however, resolve upon so decided a course of conduct, and accomplished nothing. When threats were made that Mr. Lincoln should not be inaugurated unless certain concessions were made by the Republican party, Mr. Chase responded with four words, which were at the time quite a rallying cry: "Inauguration first, adjustment afterward." The inauguration took place accordingly, and Mr. Chase was appointed Secretary of the Treasury. This appointment had been offered to him by Mr. Lincoln a little after his election, but he had not accepted, feeling disinclined to exchange his senatorship for the management of a financial concern with such very doubtful and disorderly prospects as those of the Treasury. His nomination was, however, sent in to the Senate, as it happened in his absence, and was at once confirmed unanimously. On returning and finding what had happened, he went at once to Mr. Lincoln to have the work undone. But Mr. Lincoln insisted upon it that he must stay, and so did several of his most valued friends, and he consented.

His management of the finances of the United States during the beginning and main stress of the rebellion was remarkably successful, and his money policy has been substantially followed by his successors. He raised by one loan after another, the money needed for the rapidly increasing land and sea forces of the United States, until the suspension of specie payment by the banks of the country at the end of 1861 showed that the end of the supply available from the existing financial organization of the country had been reached. He then carried into operation, with some difficulty and some resistance, the plan of issuing a legal-tender United States currency, and of organizing the banking interest so that it should be forced to use United States bonds as a basis of business, having its own notes clothed with a national character in return. These two arrangements, together with the skillful negotia-

tion of subsequent loans, carried the United States safe
through the war so far as the supply of money was
concerned, and effected something else besides. The
plan caused the money interest—indeed, the money existence—of the banks and the Government to be absolutely identical; and without doubting the patriotism
of the capitalists of the United States, it can well be
believed that they would not feel any less interest in
the success of a cause in which all, or almost all, their
means were thus ingeniously invested.

When Mr. Chase resigned the secretaryship of the
Treasury, June 30, 1864, the work to which he had set
his hand was either completed, or so distinctly planned
that other hands could continue it. In the summer of
that year he for the second time declined to allow himself to be nominated for President, not wishing to head
an opposition to Mr. Lincoln.

On the 12th of October following died Roger B.
Taney, Chief-Justice of the United States, and on the
6th of December following, Mr. Lincoln appointed Mr.
Chase to that high position. He accepted it, and now
fills it. Mr. Lincoln had intended to make this appointment in case of the death of the aged previous incumbent, ever since his accession to the Presidency.
And it was one which combined in a very rare degree
fitness of personal selection and striking poetical justice.
It was most just that the highest legal place in the
land, so long the very impregnable citadel and arsenal
of the slave power, the place whence issued the ungod-
ly Dred Scott decision, should now be occupied by that
" promising young man who had just ruined himself,"
by vainly striving to secure freedom to a miserable

negro girl more than a quarter of a century before, and who had been fighting ever since a battle seemingly hopeless against the doctrines and decisions which he was now to be able to contradict and reverse. It is scarcely possible to imagine a more completely perfect picture of a noble revenge than Salmon Portland Chase delivering judgments on the side of freedom from the chair of Roger Brooke Taney.

VII.
CALEB BLOOD SMITH.

SECRETARY SMITH, of the Interior, appears in Mr. Carpenter's picture as the tall and personable gentleman who stands behind the table, at Mr. Lincoln's left hand. With him is the thin and upright form of Mr. Blair, Postmaster-General. Caleb Blood Smith was a native of Massachusetts, having been born in Boston, April 16, 1808. When he was a boy of six, his parents removed to Cincinnati, Ohio, which was in that day "The Far West." Young Smith went through college in Ohio, beginning his course at Cincinnati College, and graduating at Miami University, and after studying law was admitted to the bar and opened an office at Connersville, Indiana. Hon. O. H. Smith, himself subsequently United States senator from Indiana, was the lawyer with whom the future Secretary studied. He thus relates their first interview, and his opinions of his student.

"One day I was sitting in my office at Connersville, when there entered a small youth, about five feet eight inches high, large head, thin brown hair, light blue eyes, high, capacious forehead and good features, and introduced himself as Caleb B. Smith, from Cincinnati. He stated his business in a lisping tone. He had come to read law with me if I would receive him. I assented to his wishes, and he remained with me until he was admitted to practice, and commenced his professional as well as political career at Connersville. He rose rapidly at the bar, was remarkably fluent, rapid, and eloquent before the jury, never at a loss for ideas or words to express them; if he had a fault as an advocate, it was that he suffered his nature to press forward his ideas, for utterance faster than the minds of the jurors were prepared to receive them; still, he was very successful before the court and jury. He was one of the most eloquent and powerful speakers in the United States."

Mr. Smith early turned his attention to political life, and became an influential member of the Whig party in Indiana, serving in the Legislature of that State during the four consecutive years from 1833 to 1836, and being Speaker of the House in 1835 and 1836. In 1840 he was one of the Whig electors who voted for General Harrison for President, and during his State political career he also held the responsible financial public office of State Fund Commissioner for Indiana. He was a member of Congress from the fourth district of the State during that interesting period from 1843 to 1847, being the last part of Mr. Tyler's administration and the first part of Mr. Polk's, when the Oregon question, with its alliterative war-cry of "Fifty-four forty, or fight!" stirred the country up so thoroughly about England, and when the annexation of Texas and the subsequent Mexican war showed so plainly how bold, how large, and how dishonest were the plans in operation to "extend the area of freedom" for the use of slavery. Mr. Smith's course in Congress was one of creditable and consistent co-operation with his party. His efficiency as a working member caused him to be appointed after the war as Commissioner of the Board for adjusting war-claims against Mexico; and having completed this task, he established himself at Cincinnati in the practice of the law.

When the Republican party was organized, Mr. Smith joined it, and was on the Ohio Fremont electoral ticket in 1856. Two years later, in 1858, he removed again to Indianapolis, and was there in practice at the bar when appointed by Mr. Lincoln Secretary of the Interior. This office was originally suggested in the session of 1848-9, by Mr. R. J. Walker, then Secretary of the Treasury, who found his own hands overloaded with work. It includes the care of Patents, Public Lands, the accounts of U. S. Marshals and other law officers, Indian Affairs, Pensions, the Census, Public Buildings, etc., being a department for the home and domestic business of the United States. The law creating it was passed March 3, 1849, and Hon. Thomas Ewing was the first Secretary. Mr. Smith had long been a political and personal friend of Mr. Lincoln, and was appointed with full knowledge of his fitness for the place.

In this responsible and important trust Secretary Smith labored steadily and successfully, until his appointment to be U. S. Judge for the District of Indiana, which was confirmed by the Senate, December 22, 1862; and he was succeeded in his place at Washington by Hon. John P. Usher, also an Indianian, Jan. 8, 1863. Judge Smith died only a few months after his appointment, leaving an unspotted personal and official reputation.

VIII.

GIDEON WELLES.

The grave, reflective features, long beard, and wig of Secretary Welles are familiar to most persons, so extensively has his portrait been placed before the public, either in earnest or in jest. In Mr. Carpenter's picture he sits beyond the table, at Mr. Lincoln's left hand, between him and the group of Messrs. Smith, Blair, and Bates.

Mr. Welles descends from one of the oldest Puritan stocks, being the sixth in direct descent from Thomas Welles, Governor of Connecticut in 1655 and 1658. The Secretary's brother, Thaddeus, still occupies the same farm in Glastenbury which their ancestor the Puritan Governor bought of Sowheag, the great Indian sachem at Middletown, two hundred years ago. This is a long time, in a country of cheap conveyances of land, for real estate to remain in the same family. Mr. Welles' father lived to be 80; his grandfather to be 73; his great-grandfather to be 86; and the next ancestor back to be 72. The wives of these stout old gentlemen lived to about the same age; so that the Secretary has a sort of inherited right to live long.

The father of the Secretary was a thrifty and respectable Glastenbury farmer, and gave his son a good education. The boy, after some experience in the district school, was sent to the Episcopal Academy at Cheshire, near New Haven, and afterward to Norwich

University, Vermont, which was first established as a
military school, in 1820, by Captain Alden Partridge,
the well-known soldier and teacher. For some reason
or other, however, young Welles did not graduate there,
but returned to his native State and established himself in Hartford, which has remained his residence ever
since, except at the two periods when he has held office
in Washington. Here he studied law under Chief-
Justice Williams and Judge W. W. Ellsworth. But his
natural inclination was much stronger toward politics
and political literature than toward the more plodding
legal industry of the courts; and not having become
very deeply immersed in the practice of law, he found
it easy and agreeable, in 1826, to become a proprietor
and the editor of the Hartford *Times*, a paper which,
whether its politics have been right or wrong, has always been conducted with shrewdness, energy, and
power, and is so still. It was when Mr. Welles became
connected with it the recognized organ of the Democratic party in Connecticut, and it is an influential
organ of that party now.

As editor of the *Times*, or as a principal writer for
it, Mr. Welles exerted a powerful influence in the politics of his State, and to some extent in national politics. This influence was in great measure exerted in
consultation with Hon. John M. Niles, for three terms
United States senator from Connecticut, and in his day
the leader of his party in his State. So complete was
his control over the Democracy supposed to be, that
" Niles's cattle" was one of the regular sneers almost
every day cast at the " Locofocos" by their Whig ad-
versaries. It was Mr. Niles who was foremost in es-

tablishing the *Times*, in 1817, and until Mr. Welles took his place he was principal editor.

Messrs. Niles and Welles were both devoted partisans of General Jackson, and the *Times* was the first newspaper that urged his election to the Presidency of the United States; it stuck to him through evil and good report until his election in 1828, and was a most thorough and effective supporter of his administration from beginning to end.

In 1827 Mr. Welles was elected to the State Legislature, and was re-elected yearly until 1835; and as he resigned his editorial chair at the end of General Jackson's second term, his chief activity as a State legistor and politician may perhaps be placed within that period of eight years. During this time he was a most vigorous adversary to a scheme then proposed to prohibit from giving evidence in courts persons not believing in a future state of rewards and punishments; he labored perseveringly to abolish imprisonment for debt, which he finally succeeded in doing; he advocated and carried the enactment of general laws for the establishment of business corporations, in place of the previous practice of legislating specially for each new company; and in the days when a silver quarter of a dollar was the postage on "each sheet or piece of paper," and long before the public at large were thinking about it, he set on foot an important agitation for cheap and uniform postage. The mere statement of these "heads of controversy" shows the genuine "democracy" in the real, not the partisan political sense of the word, of Mr. Welles' views.

In 1835 Mr. Welles was controller of public ac-

11

counts of the State; in 1836 he was made postmaster at Hartford, and retained the office until removed under Harrison's administration in 1841; in 1842 he was controller again; and in 1846, President Polk, without any previous notice, offered him an appointment as Chief of the Bureau of Provisions and Clothing in the Navy Department at Washington. This office he accepted, and retained until 1849.

Mr. Welles, as a Democrat, had always been an admirer of Jefferson, and in accordance with the views of that statesman, he was unconditionally opposed to the extension of slave territory. When, therefore, the annexation of Texas, the Mexican War, the contest over Mr. Clay's compromise, and the other measures connected with these, showed that the Democratic party was ceasing to be the progressive party and becoming a retrogressive one—was changing from the party of human rights into a machine for promoting slavery, he necessarily felt himself repelled from it—a feeling, by the way, in which his old friend Senator Niles most fully sympathized. Both of them, although they had not united with the Liberty party nor the Free-soil party, joined heartily in the organization of the Republican party in 1855; Mr. Welles was the candidate of the new party for Governor of Connecticut in 1856; and on the establishment in the same year of the Hartford *Evening Press* as the organ of the new party, he transferred his counsels and his pen to the new paper. He was soon appointed a member of the Republican National Committee, and at the Chicago Convention in 1860 which nominated Mr. Lincoln, Mr. Welles was chairman of the Connecticut delegation.

During Mr. Lincoln's tour in the East, in the beginning
of 1860, Mr. Welles was much with him; and doubtless may then have formed such an opinion of his Connecticut companion as induced the subsequent selection
of him for Secretary of the Navy. The writer of the
present sketch very well remembers being in the State
Library at Hartford one day when Mr. Welles and
Mr. Lincoln entered together, and smiling to see the tall
form of Mr. Welles so effectually out-topped by the
lengthy Illinoian. It was not then generally foreseen
that Mr. Lincoln would be President, Mr. Seward being
the choice more usually expected; and yet it is not
improbable that the experienced campaigner of the
times of Jackson and Van Buren may already have
speculated, in his own peculiarly silent and quiet manner, upon the chances of Illinois as against New York.
And if Illinois were to be the nominating State, it followed of course that Mr. Lincoln would be the man.
Be that as it may, Mr. Welles was appointed Secretary
of the Navy, and was retained in that place by Mr.
Lincoln's successor. His administration of his very important trust has been often assailed for a variety of
reasons. Whatever the occasion or the violence of those
attacks, Mr. Welles has answered none of them. This
is not the place for any discussion of such matters; but
it may properly be remarked that the United States
Navy during the rebellion was of gigantic size and
importance, far beyond comparison with its condition
at any previous period; and further, that its growth, efficiency, economy, and good management under Mr.
Welles will bear comparison with those of any other
department of the Government during the same period.

IX.

EDWIN M. STANTON.

MR. STANTON was the youngest man of President Lincoln's cabinet, having been born at Steubenville, Ohio, in 1815. His family, like those of Mr. Lincoln and Attorney-General Bates, was of Quaker descent. His parents had removed to Ohio from Culpepper County, Virginia, where his mother's father once owned the ground on which was fought the battle of Cedar Mountain, August 9, 1862, between Banks and Stonewall Jackson. After an ordinary preparatory training, he entered Kenyon College in 1833, but remained only a year; after that time he became a bookseller's clerk at Columbus, Ohio, but at the same time studied law under L. D. Collier, Esq., and was admitted to the bar in 1836. He began practice at Cadiz, in Harrison County, and almost immediately attracted attention as a lawyer of ability. In the next year, 1837, he was chosen prosecuting attorney of the county. Soon afterwards he established himself in Steubenville, where he very quickly attained an extensive business. In 1839 he became official reporter of the decisions of the Supreme Court of Ohio, and so remained during three years. By this time Mr. Stanton's reputation was very high throughout all southeast Ohio and the neighboring part of Virginia, both for arguing questions of law and for power in convincing juries. While established here, he went to Washington to defend C. J. McNulty, of Ohio, clerk of the House of, Representatives, on trial upon a charge of embezzlement in office, and succeeded in securing his acquittal.

While thus at work in his profession, he was also an energetic and efficient politician, laboring vigorously in the ranks of the Democratic party. In 1848, as his reputation caused him to be employed in more and more important causes, he removed to Pittsburg, as a better center of operations, and remained until 1857. Here Mr. Stanton speedily became the acknowledged leader of the bar, and began to be employed in many heavy and important cases before the United States Supreme Court at Washington. One of these, the Wheeling Bridge case, involved the same important and violently and repeatedly contested question that has frequently arisen in similar cases, whether the convenience of the land routes or of the water routes shall be served, when a bridge is wanted over a navigable stream. No lawsuits are fought with more energy, anger, and force than these. This fact is easy to understand when it is considered that they necessarily occur between parties of large means, and of that peculiar obstinate, powerful, aggressive executive energy of character that belongs to the promoters of great industrial and social enterprises. Mr. Stanton's vast endowment of exactly those qualities rendered him a sympathetic and interested lawyer for just such men; and his argument in the Wheeling case is perhaps the best known of all his legal efforts.

In 1857, Mr. Stanton removed again from Pittsburg to the still larger arena of Washington, where he quickly entered into the peculiar and lucrative patent department of law practice. During the year after his removal to Washington, he was selected by Attorney-General Black to go to California to argue for the United States some land cases involving principles and values of very great importance, which came up before the California State courts.

Late in the year 1860, after the secession of South Carolina, great difficulties and vexations arose within the Cabinet of Mr. Buchanan, from the operation of the existing political troubles, and from the clashing views, purposes, and characters of the members of the Government. Hon. Lewis Cass, then Secretary of State, unable to control the course of events or to endure the machinations of the dishonest officials around him, resigned his place on the 14th of December, and Attorney-General Black was appointed in his stead. Mr. Stanton, well known hitherto as a Democrat in politics, and as a prompt, energetic, and able lawyer, was appointed to the vacant post of Attorney-General, and as such he bore a part in the disturbed and uneasy remainder of Mr. Buchanan's administration. The details of this portion of his career are known only to himself and his fellow-members of the Cabinet. But he took a strong and determined position in defence of the United States, and of the dignities and rights of the central government, as against the feeble and wailing acquiescence of Mr. Buchanan, and one or two of the Cabinet, and against the monstrous and impudent treasons of the rest of it. In a conversation with Mr. Carpenter, Mr. Stanton once gave the following brief glimpse into that sufficiently contemptible interior:

" This little incident," said Stanton, speaking of Major

Anderson's removal to Fort Sumter, " was the crisis of our history—the pivot upon which everything turned. Had he remained in Fort Moultrie, a very different combination of circumstances would have arisen. The attack on Sumter—commenced by the South—united the North, and made the success of the Confederacy impossible. I shall never forget," he continued, " our coming together by special summons that night. Buchanan sat in his arm-chair in a corner of the room, white as a sheet, with the stump of a cigar in his mouth. The dispatches were laid before us; and so much violence ensued, that he had to turn us all out-of-doors."

Upon Mr. Lincoln's accession, Mr. Cameron was appointed Secretary of War; and upon his resigning January 14, 1862, to accept the appointment of envoy extraordinary and minister plenipotentiary to Russia, Mr. Stanton was appointed to the vacant secretaryship on the 20th of the same month. It was with a just consciousness of his powers of straightforward hard work, of judicious organization, and of selecting and controlling men, that he accepted the place, yet with no vain-glory, nor with any idle under-estimate of the problem to be solved. He had not been a member of the Republican party, but a thorough Jacksonian Democrat. Still, Mr. Seward, Mr. Chase, and Mr. Cameron himself were all well aware of the remarkable energy, fearlessness, force of will, and unqualified patriotism shown in his position in the Buchanan Cabinet. They knew that he, with Judge Holt and General Dix, had substantially preserved the Government; that had it not been for those three men, doubtless the whole frame of the administration would have been knocked out of the trembling and feeble hands of Mr. Buchanan, to be broken into splinters, or to be grasped and controlled by the Southern traitors of that Cabinet. When Mr. Stanton went to the White House to receive his commission from Mr. Lincoln, the President and he had never seen each other. It is said also that Mr. Stanton had no notice whatever of the intended appointment until the day before his nomination was sent to the Senate, the information being given to him just as he was about to argue a cause before the Supreme Court. In a brief article on Mr. Stanton which appeared some time ago in *Harper's Weekly*, and which is understood to have been written by an intimate personal and political friend, the writer says: "The relations thus commenced between the President and the Secretary of War always remained exceedingly cordial, or rather, they constantly became warmer and more confidential, down to the last fatal day which ended Mr. Lincoln's earthly career. While he was rarely seen at the offices of the other executive departments, at the War Office he was not merely a frequent but a constant visitor. His tall form, wrapped in his familiar gray shawl, was usually to be seen making its way along the back alley that leads there from the White House, at from nine to ten o'clock in the morning, or about four in the afternoon; and persons who were admitted to see the Secretary on important business in his private room at those hours would sometimes find the President stretched upon the sofa there, as if the discussion between him and the Secretary had not yet been concluded. Indeed, the tie between them seemed to be quite as much that of private affection as of official duty; and when the catastrophe occurred which robed the nation in mourning, all will remember how admirably the confidence of the deceased statesman in his friend and adviser was justified by the latter. For a brief time, in that awful crisis, the whole government seemed to rest upon the shoulders of the Secretary of War, and the country will not soon forget the manner in which the momentous trust was discharged."

Mr. Lincoln, besides proceeding upon the recommendations of the other secretaries, chose Mr. Stanton with a wise consideration of geography. In answering some questions on the subject, he observed that his first wish had been to choose a man from a border State, but that he knew New England would object; that on the other hand he would have also been glad to choose a New Englander, but he knew the Border States would object. So, on the whole, he concluded to select from some intervening territory; "and to tell you the truth, gentlemen," he added, " I don't believe Stanton knows where he belongs himself." Some of the company now said something about Mr. Stanton's impulsiveness, to which Mr. Lincoln replied with one of those queer stories with which he used to answer friends and enemies alike. " Well," he said, " we may have to treat him as they are sometimes obliged to treat a Methodist minister I know of out West. He gets wrought up so high in his prayers and exhortations that they are obliged to put bricks in his pockets to keep him down. We may be obliged to serve Stanton the same way, but I guess we'll let him jump awhile first!"

An interesting anecdote was a short time since printed in the Cincinnati *Gazette*, illustrating well the complete confidence existing between the President and his Secretary of War.

" While the President," says this account, " was on his way back from Richmond, and at a point where no. telegraph could reach the steamer upon which he was, a dispatch of the utmost importance reached Washington, demanding the immediate decision of the President himself. The dispatch was received by a confidential staff officer, who at once ascertained that Mr. Lincoln could not be reached. Delay was out of the question, as important army movements were involved. The officer having the dispatch went with it directly to Mr. Stanton's office, but the Secretary could not be found. Messengers were hastily dispatched for him in all directions. Their search was useless, and a positive answer had been already too much delayed by the time it had occupied. With great reluctance the staff officer sent a reply in the President's name. Soon after Mr. Stanton entered himself, having learned of the efforts made to find him. The dispatch was produced, and he was informed by the officer sending the answer, of what had been done.

" 'Did I do right?' said the officer to the Secretary.

" 'Yes, Major,' replied Mr. Stanton, 'I think you have sent the correct reply, but I should hardly have dared to take the responsibility.'

" At this the whole magnitude of the office, and the great responsibility he had taken upon himself, seemed to fall upon the officer, and almost overcame him, and he asked Mr. Stanton what he had better do, and was advised to go directly to the President, on his return, and state the case frankly to him. It was a sleepless night for this officer, and at the very earliest hour consistent with propriety he went to the White House, Mr. Lincoln having returned late the night before, but was refused admission by the usher, who told him·that the President had given strict orders to admit no one upon any pretense till after a certain hour. In vain did the officer urge ·the importahce of his errand; the usher would not take in his name, and he was about turning away when the President's son came down stairs, bade the officer good-morning, and, on hearing he had been refused admission, said that his father would certainly see the Major. Still the usher was not to be moved, till the son went back himself, and returned with the message that the President would see him.

"Mr. Lincoln was reclining on a lounge as the officer entered, looking over a pile of papers. He appeared a little annoyed at the interruption, but stopped at once to hear his visitor's mission. The dispatch was shown him, and the action upon it stated frankly and briefly. The President thought a moment and then said, 'Did you consult the Secretary of War, Major?' The absence of the Secretary at the important moment was then related to Mr. Lincoln, with the subsequent remark of Mr. Stanton that he thought the right answer had been given, but that he himself would have shrunk from the responsibility.

"Mr. Lincoln, on hearing the story, rose, crossed the room, and taking the officer by the hand thanked him cordially, and then' spoke earnestly of Mr. Stanton as follows: 'Hereafter, Major, *whenever you have Mr. Stanton's sanction in any matter, you have mine, for so great is my confidence in his judgment and patriot-ism, that I never wish to take an important step my-self without first consulting him.'* "

The story of life within the Cabinet during the war is varied with all manner of friendly and unfriendly colorings; but on the whole it is a fine picture of strong and decided men striving to do their best for the country, and to postpone or reconcile personal ob-jects and sentiments so far as they interfered with the common object. Very many of its inside occurrences have all the hearty friendliness of events in a family of grown-up, positive, but kindly brothers. Mr. Car-penter tells a graphic anecdote of the strong regard of Mr. Lincoln for Secretary Stanton. "A few days be-fore the President's death," he says, " Secretary Stan-ton tendered his resignation of the War Department. He accompanied the act with a heart-felt tribute to Mr. Lincoln's constant friendship and faithful devotion to the country,; saying, also, that he as Secretary had ac-cepted the position to hold it only until the war should end, and that now he felt his work was done, and his duty was to resign.

" Mr. Lincoln was greatly moved by the Secretary's words, and tearing in pieces the paper containing the resignation, and throwing his arms about the Secretary, he said: ' Stanton, you have been a good friend and a faithful public servant, and it is not for you to say when you will no longer be needed here.' Several friends of both parties were present on the occasion, and there was not a dry eye that witnessed the scene."

At the Cabinet meeting which Mr. Carpenter once attended, Mr. Usher, then Secretary of the Interior, told Mr. Stanton that he had a young friend whom he wished to have appointed a paymaster in the army. "How old is he?" asked Mr. Stanton, gruffly. "About twenty-one, I believe," answered Mr. Usher; "he is of good family and excellent character. "Usher," exclaimed Mr. Stanton, in reply, "I would not appoint the Angel Gabriel a paymaster if he was only twenty-one."

A good instance of the kind of influence which Mr. Stanton exerted upon the war, and of the way he used it, is given in the account of a correspondent of the Boston *Commonwealth*, of the occasion when negotiation upon political matters was forbidden to General Grant. It was at the capital, on the night of March 3d, 1865, and while the last bills from Congress were being read and signed, and the accounts from Grant of the certain speedy destruction of Lee's army were being discussed, that, the story says, "Mr. Lincoln was elated, and the kindness of his heart was manifest in intimations of favorable terms to be granted to the conquered rebels.

"Stanton listened in silence, restraining his emotion, but at length the tide burst forth. 'Mr. President,' said he, 'to-morrow is inauguration day. If you are not to be the President of an obedient and united people, you had better not be inaugurated. Your work is already done, if any other authority than yours is for one moment to be recognized, or any terms made that do not signify you are the supreme head of the nation. If generals in the field are to negotiate peace, or any other chief magistrate is to be acknowledged on this continent, then you are not needed, and you had better not take the oath of office.'

" 'Stanton, you are right!' said the President, his whole tone changing. 'Let me have a pen.'

" Mr. Lincoln sat down at the table, and wrote as follows:

" 'The President directs me to say to you that he wishes you to have no conference with General Lee, unless it be for the capitulation of Lee's army, or on some minor or purely military matter. He instructs me to say that you are not to decide, discuss, or confer upon any political question. Such questions the President holds in his own hands, and will submit them to no military conferences or conventions. In the mean time you are to press to the utmost your military advantages.'

" The President read over what he had written, and then said:

" 'Now, Stanton, date and sign this paper, and send it to Grant. We'll see about this peace business.'

" The duty was discharged only too gladly by the energetic and far-sighted Secretary; with what effect and renown the country knows full well."

Mr. Stanton's official doings as Secretary of War have been very often and very violently attacked, and charges of every sort, from oppression, cruelty, and official brutality to the grossest and vilest malfeasance and corruption, have been made against him. None of these, however, have ever lived long enough to produce an impression upon the public, and Mr. Stanton himself has treated them with utter neglect. This disregard of cotemporary personal reputation was a habit of his before he became Secretary; for he never took pains to preserve any of his legal productions, and the personal friend who prepared the sketch of Mr. Stanton, above quoted from, says : " In one of these cases, which related to the right of the Suspension Bridge Company, at Wheeling, to construct their bridge across the Ohio River, his plea is spoken of by those who had the luck to hear it as a most remarkable performance, but we have not succeeded in procuring a printed copy of it."

We quote from the same paper its very well-outlined sketch of Mr. Stanton's personal appearance :

" Mr. Stanton is about five feet eight inches in height, and is a person of broad shoulders and heavy frame. His features are rather round and full, his hair very dark, though thin, and his complexion sallow. These peculiarities, combined with his intense and penetrating dark brown eyes, and his heavy beard sprinkled freely with gray, give somewhat of an Oriental air to his general appearance. Though his ordinary expression is thoughtful, absorbed, and stern, his smile is gentle and winning as a woman's."

In an enthusiastic account of the Secretary of War, printed some time ago in the *Illinois State Journal*, is given the following picture of his character as a business man : " His mind never ceases to act, and his body is never fatigued with executing. The former never rests, and the latter never bends beneath its work. The writer, when a boy, used to study in a room under his office, and knows that he was accustomed to work all day and until the small hours of the night began their increase. His industry would astonish ordinary men, and the amount of work which he did could never have been endured by other than a man of iron. When immersed in business and surrounded by a multitude of details he seemed at home—confusion under his energy soon became system. He seemed always posted in his business, he never took up a wrong paper, turned to a wrong page, or read a wrong extract. His memory never deserted him, and his judgment never erred."

Mr. Stanton has been twice married, his present wife having been a Miss Ellen Dickinson of Pittsburg. By his first marriage he has a son, now about twenty-five years of age; and by his second, a son and two daughters, all yet quite young.

X.

EDWARD BATES.

JUDGE BATES was born in Goochland County, Virginia—a county in the heart of the State, on the north bank of James River, and next above Henrico, in which stands the city of Richmond—in 1793. His family had been Quakers, but his father, after the fashion of the sect, had been cast out of it for bearing arms during the Revolution. The education of the boy was conducted under the supervision of a relative of much culture; and about 1814 he removed to Missouri in company with his elder brother, Frederick, appointed Secretary of the Territory under the well-known Western explorer Governor William Clark, and afterward in 1824 himself elected Governor of the State. St. Louis, where the young man established himself, was then a town of less than 5,000 inhabitants, and the whole Territory numbered not more than about 50,000 souls.

Mr. Bates very soon became eminent as a lawyer possessing excellent judgment, ample knowledge, and much power of calm and deliberate argument. When, on July 19, 1820, the convention to frame a State constitution met at St. Louis, Mr. Bates was an influential member of it, and was for a long time a leading member of the Territorial and afterward of the State Legislature. During the Twentieth Congress, 1827–9, he served as a representative in Congress from Missouri.

12

Mr. Bates found political life well suited to his tastes and acquirements, but the state of his private fortune did not allow him to pursue such a career, and accordingly at the end of his Congressional term he went quietly home to his law practice in St. Louis. Here he labored faithfully and obscurely, well known within his own State, but very little out of it, until the Internal Improvement Convention of 1847, which met at Chicago. To this assembly Mr. Bates was a delegate, and here he astonished the Convention by delivering a speech upon the question before them, so powerful, eloquent, and conclusive, as to fill his audience with surprise and delight. An attempt was quickly made to enlist so much ability in the service of the Whig party; but Mr. Bates persistently declined either to accept any State office, or to take the Secretaryship which President Fillmore offered him.

On questions of national policy Mr. Bates was a follower of Henry Clay. On the subject of slavery he had excellent opportunities for forming his opinions, as. the admission of his State to the Union was the occasion of the Missouri Compromise. The debates attending that measure had powerfully discussed the subject, and it had naturally been considered and argued fully within the State whose existence as a State was brought into question. Mr. Bates was by natural constitution of mind a conservative, but he was also a fearless and just man. While he was far from holding the views of the political abolitionists, he was still decidedly an emancipationist of the school of Henry Clay; and he exemplified his beliefs on the subject by manumitting his own slaves. When the question of the repeal of the Missouri Compromise came up, he was energetic and thorough in his opposition to it; and from that time forward he labored for the party of freedom in Missouri, taking the ground that free labor was right in itself, and was far more profitable to the State. He was also a firm opponent of the whole series of measures pursued by Mr. Buchanan's administration toward the infant State of Kansas.

At the Chicago Convention to nominate a Republican candidate for the Presidency, in 1860, Mr. Bates was the favorite candidate of many members, both from the West and East. Upon Mr. Lincoln's election, Mr. Bates' appointment to the place of Attorney-General was the very first of the Cabinet appointments definitely determined upon. His course while a Cabinet officer was marked by entire personal good feeling toward Mr. Lincoln, and by a steady and cautious official conservatism; while his earnest and resolute Unionism was never doubted nor questioned. After Mr. Lincoln's re-election, Mr. Bates resigned his post, as he had once before retired from political life, for reasons personal to himself, and not in accordance with any desire of Mr. Lincoln's, and once more returned to his home at St. Louis, where he has since remained in private life.

XI.

MONTGOMERY BLAIR.

POSTMASTER-GENERAL MONTGOMERY BLAIR is in the third generation of his family who have been prominent in political life.* About the year 1800, in the days of the violent political warfare between the Federalists and the Republicans, and when Kentucky was still harassed along her borders by the Indians, whose warfare had given it the name of "The Dark and Bloody Ground," James Blair, a Virginian of Scotch descent, was living at Abingdon, Washington County, Virginia, a small town in the southwestern corner of that State, on the head waters of the Holston River, and in the district so well known during the war for the Union, as the scene of one of those adventurous and damaging cavalry raids which struck so sharply and deeply into the heart of the rebellion. Mr. Blair removed to Kentucky, taking with him a son, Francis Preston Blair, then about ten years old. Mr. James Blair became an influential politician, and was at one time attorney-general of Kentucky.

Francis P. Blair, the son, was educated at Transylvania University, and was a partisan of Henry Clay in 1824, but soon afterward became an advocate of General Jackson's views.

In the winter of 1830-1, President Jackson discovered that the leading party "organ," the *Telegraph*, though still professedly his advocate, was about to go over to the side of Mr. Calhoun, who was then just appearing in Congress as the leader of the nullification scheme. During the previous summer, a gentleman had casually shown the President an article in the Frankfort *Argus*, a Kentucky paper, containing a strong review of a late nullification speech in Congress. The President, much pleased with the power of the article, had inquired who wrote it, and was told, Mr. Francis P. Blair. When, therefore, he found out the proposed desertion of his allies of the *Telegraph*, he caused a proposition to be made to the Kentuckian, to come and establish a Jackson paper in Washington. Mr. Blair, holding a well-paid position as clerk of the Kentucky Circuit Court, being also the president of the Commonwealth Bank with a salary, and owning also a good plantation, had supposed himself permanently established, and was entirely taken by surprise by this application. Being, however, an ardent friend of General Jackson's policy, he very soon gave up his Kentucky interests, came to Washington, and established that famous newspaper the *Globe*. John C. Rives was soon afterward associated with him in the management of the new paper; and the important part which it played under their management in the disturbed and violent political contests of thirty years ago is matter of history. The *Congressional Globe*, a sort of successor of the *Globe*, is still regularly issued at Washington; and the important though unobtrusive influence exerted by Mr. Blair both in those days and even down to the period of the rebellion, as a shrewd and trusted adviser of the managers of the Democratic

party, is perhaps as well known as the fame of the
newspaper which he edited.

Mr. Blair controlled the *Globe* until Mr. Polk became
President, when Mr. Ritchie was put in his place. On
being afterward urged to resume the place, he declined;
he also declined an offer of the mission to Spain, and
an offer of some other diplomatic appointment for his
son, and took up his abode at a country seat called
Silver Spring, in Maryland, where he has resided ever
since, busying himself with farming when not employed
in politics. Mr. Blair supported the Van Buren or
Free-soil Democratic movement in 1848, and the Fremont movement in 1856.

Montgomery Blair, son of the editor of the *Globe*,
was born in Kentucky, May 10, 1813. He studied at
West Point, where he graduated at the age of 22, and
being according to custom commissioned as second
lieutenant, he served in the Seminole war. After
about a year's soldiering, however, he resigned, and
settled at St. Louis, as a lawyer, in 1837. Here he
was prosperous in law and in politics, holding at various times, during the period from 1839 to 1849, the
offices of United States District Attorney, Judge of the
Court of Common Pleas, and Mayor of the city. In
1852 Mr. Blair removed to Maryland, where he established himself in his father's neighborhood, in a house
called Montgomery Castle.   ·

Mr. Blair, like his father, was a Jacksonian Democrat; but when the Missouri Compromise was repealed
he cast in his lot with the Republican party. Upon
this, President Buchanan promptly removed him from
the solicitorship of the Court of Claims, a post given

him by Mr. Pierce. Mr. Blair, like his father and brother, is a thorough politician, and also like them is a man of strong and unconditional likes and dislikes, and prompt and decided in action. Moreover, the father and the two sons very naturally and properly co-operated with each other in advice, influence, and management. Accordingly, they were all more or less interested in the appointment of General Fremont to Missouri, and afterward in his removal. Mr. Montgomery Blair and his brother F. P. Blair had both been active and influential St. Louis politicians also, and thus they were pretty intimately mixed up with the peculiarly turbulent and passionate politics of Missouri and Kansas during the war. These experiences necessarily procured them enemies, and these enemies worked hard to procure Mr. Blair's ejection from the postmastership. So much hostile feeling at last grew up within the Republican party on the subject, that Mr. Blair, with correct and manly feeling, requested Mr. Lincoln to tell him when to resign, and he would do so. The President accordingly requested it, September 23, 1864, and the resignation was offered and accepted accordingly. The correspondence is so creditable to both parties, and so brief, that we give it in full:

EXECUTIVE MANSION, WASHINGTON, *September* 23, 1864.
HON. MONTGOMERY BLAIR:

My Dear Sir :—You have generously said to me, more than once, that whenever your resignation could be a relief to me, it was at my disposal. The time has come. You very well know that this proceeds from no dissatisfaction of mine with you personally or officially. Your uniform kindness has been unsurpassed by that of any other friend, and while it is true that the war does not so greatly add to the difficulties of your department as to those of some others, it is yet much to say, as I most truly can, that in the three years and a half during which you have administered the General Post-Office, I remember no single complaint against you in connection therewith.

Yours, as ever,　　　　　　　A. LINCOLN.

MR. BLAIR'S REPLY.

My Dear Sir :—I have received your note of this date, referring to my offers to resign whenever you should deem it advisable for the public interest that I should do so, and stating that, in your judgment, that time has now come. I now, therefore, formally tender my resignation of the office of Postmaster-General. I can not take leave of you without renewing the expressions of my gratitude for the uniform kindness which has marked your course toward,

Yours truly,　　　　　M. BLAIR.

THE PRESIDENT.

The four years' term of office thus filled by Mr. Blair was by the nature of his occupation far less calculated to keep him prominently before the public, than the Secretaryships of War, of the Navy, and of the Treasury. In them success draws attention, but the better the Post-Office Department is managed the less will be said about it. This Department was conducted with decided ability by Mr. Blair, and the fewness of complaints against his administration of it is equivalent to high positive praise.

APPENDIX.

PROCLAMATION OF EMANCIPATION.

I, ABRAHAM LINCOLN, President of the United States, and Commander-in-chief of the Army and Navy thereof, do hereby proclaim and declare that hereafter, as heretofore, the war will be prosecuted for the object of practically restoring the constitutional relation between the United States and the people thereof in those States in which that relation is, or may be, suspended or disturbed; that it is my purpose upon the next meeting of Congress to again recommend the adoption of a practical measure tendering pecuniary aid to the free acceptance or rejection of all the Slave States, so-called, the people whereof may not then be in rebellion against the United States, and which States may then have voluntarily adopted, or thereafter may voluntarily adopt, the immediate or gradual abolishment of Slavery within their respective limits, and that the effort to colonize persons of African descent, with their consent, upon the continent or elsewhere, with the previously obtained consent of the government existing there, will be continued; that on the first day of January, in the year of our Lord one thousand eight hundred and sixty-three, all persons held as slaves within any State, or any designated part of a State, the people whereof shall then be in rebellion against the United States, SHALL BE THEN, THENCEFORWARD, AND FOREVER FREE; and the military and naval authority thereof will recognize and maintain the freedom of such persons, and will do no act or acts to repress such persons, or any of them, in any efforts they may make for actual freedom; that the Executive will, on the first day of January aforesaid, by proclamation, designate the States and parts of States, if any, in which the people thereof respectively shall then be in rebellion against the United States; and the fact that any State, or the people thereof, shall on that day be in good faith represented in the Congress of the United States by members chosen thereto, at elections wherein a majority of the qualified voters of such State shall have participated, shall, in the absence of strong countervailing testimony, be deemed conclusive evidence that such State and the people thereof have not been in rebellion against the United States.

That attention is hereby called to an act of Congress entitled, "An act to make an additional article of war," approved March 13, 1862, and which act is in the words and figures following:

"*Be it enacted by the Senate and House of Representatives of the United States of America, in Congress, assembled,* That hereafter the following shall be promulgated as an additional article of war for the government of the Army of the United States, and shall be observed and obeyed as such:

"ARTICLE —. All officers or persons of the military or naval service of the United States are prohibited from employing any of the forces under their respective commands for the purpose of returning fugitives from service or labor who may have escaped from any persons to whom such service or labor is claimed to be due, and any officer who shall be found guilty by a court-martial of violating this article, shall be dismissed from the service.

"SEC. 2. And be it further enacted, that this act shall take effect from and after its passage."

Also to the ninth and tenth sections of an act entitled, "An act to suppress insurrection, to punish treason and rebellion, to seize and confiscate property of Rebels, and for other purposes," approved July 17, 1862, and which sections are in the words and figures following:

"SEC. 9. And be it further enacted, that all slaves of persons who shall hereafter be engaged in rebellion against the Government of the United States, or who shall in any way give aid or comfort thereto, escaping from such persons and taking refuge within the lines of the army; and all slaves captured from such persons or deserted by them, and coming under the control of the Government of the United States, and all slaves of such persons found on (or being within) any place occupied by Rebel forces and afterward occupied by the forces of the United States, shall be deemed captives of war, and shall be forever free of their servitude and not again held as slaves.

"Sec. 10. And be it further enacted, that no slave escaping into any State, Territory, or the District of Columbia, from any of the States, shall be delivered up, or in any way impeded or hindered of his liberty, except for crime, or some offense against the laws, unless the person claiming said fugitive shall first make oath that the person to whom the labor or service of such fugitive is alleged to be due, is his lawful owner, and has not been in arms against the United States in the present rebellion, nor in any way given aid or comfort thereto; and no person engaged in the military or naval service of the United States shall, under any pretense whatever, assume to decide on the validity of the claim of any person to the service or labor of any other person, or surrender up any such person to the claimant, on pain of being dismissed from the service."

And I do hereby enjoin upon, and order all persons engaged in the military and naval service of the United States to observe, obey, and enforce within their respective spheres of service the act and sections above recited.

And the Executive will, in due time, recommend that all citizens of the United States who shall have remained loyal thereto throughout the rebellion, shall (upon the restoration of the constitutional relation between the United States and their respective States and people, if the relation shall have been suspended or disturbed) be compensated for all losses by acts of the United States, including the loss of slaves.

In witness whereof, I have hereunto set my hand and caused the seal of the United States to be affixed.

Done at the city of Washington, this twenty-second day of September, in the year of our Lord one thousand eight hundred and sixty-two, and of the Independence of the United States the eighty-seventh.

By the President: ABRAHAM LINCOLN.

WM. H. SEWARD, Secretary of State.

SUPPLEMENTARY PROCLAMATION.

WHEREAS, On the twenty-second day of September, in the year of our Lord one thousand eight hundred and sixty-two, a proclamation was issued by the President of the United States, containing among other things, the following, to wit:

That on the first day of January, in the year of our Lord one thousand eight hundred and sixty-three, all persons held as slaves within any State, or any designated part of a State, the people whereof shall then be in rebellion against the United States, shall be thenceforward and forever free, and the Executive Government of the United States, including the military and naval authority thereof, will recognize and maintain the freedom of such persons, and will do no act or acts to repress such persons, or any of them, in any efforts they may make for their actual freedom:

That the Executive will, on the first day of January aforesaid, by proclamation, designate the States and parts of States, if any, in which the people thereof respectively shall then be in rebellion against the United States, and the fact that any State, or the people thereof, shall on that day be in good faith represented in the Congress of the United States by members chosen thereto at elections wherein a majority of the qualified voters of such State shall have participated, shall, in the absence of strong countervailing testimony, be deemed conclusive evidence that such State and the people thereof are not then in rebellion against the United States:

Now, therefore, I, Abraham Lincoln, President of the United States, by virtue of the power in me vested as Commander-in-chief of the Army and Navy of the United States, in time of actual armed rebellion against the authority and Government of the United States, and as a fit and necessary war measure for repressing said rebellion, do, on this first day of January, in the year of our Lord one thousand eight hundred and sixty-three, and in accordance with my purpose so to do, publicly proclaimed for the full period of one hundred days from the day of the first above-mentioned order, and designate, as the States and parts of States wherein the people thereof respectively are this day in rebellion against the United States, the following, to wit: Arkansas, Texas, Louisiana, except the parishes of St. Bernard, Plaquemine, Jefferson, St. John, St. Charles, St. James, Ascension, Assumption, Terre Bonne, Lafourche, St. Mary, St. Martin, and Orleans, including the city of New Orleans, Mississippi, Alabama, Florida, Georgia, South Carolina, North Carolina, and Virginia, except the forty-eight counties designated as West Virginia, and also the counties of Berkeley, Accomac, Northampton, Elizabeth City, York, Princess Ann, and Norfolk, including the cities of Norfolk and Portsmouth, and which excepted parts are, for the present, left precisely as if this proclamation were not issued.

And by virtue of the power and for the purpose aforesaid, I do order and declare that all persons held as slaves within said designated States and parts of States are, and henceforward shall be free; and that the Executive Government of the United States, including the military and naval authorities thereof, will recognize and maintain the freedom of said persons.

And I hereby enjoin upon the people so declared to be free, to abstain from all violence, unless in necessary self-defense, and I recommend to them, that in all cases, when allowed, they labor faithfully for reasonable wages.

And I further declare and make known that such persons of suitable condition will be received into the armed service of the United States to garrison forts, positions, stations, and other places, and to man vessels of all sorts in said service.

And upon this, sincerely believed to be an act of justice, warranted by the Constitution, upon military necessity, I invoke the considerate judgment of mankind and the gracious favor of Almighty God.

In witness whereof, I have hereunto set my hand and caused the seal of the United States to be affixed.

Done at the city of Washington, this first day of January, in the year of our Lord one thousand [L. S.] eight hundred and sixty-three, and of the Independence of the United States of America, the eighty-seventh.

By the President: ABRAHAM LINCOLN.

WILLIAM H. SEWARD, Secretary of State.

www.ingramcontent.com/pod-product-compliance
Lightning Source LLC
Chambersburg PA
CBHW030603040726
47497CB00008B/2830